Annie's Quilted Mysteries™

INNOCENT UNTIL PROVEN QUILTY

DONNA KELLY

Annie's®

AnniesFiction.com

Library of Congress-in-Publication Data
Innocent Until Proven Quilty / by Donna Kelly
p. cm.
I. Title
                    2014935429

AnniesFiction.com
800-282-6643
Annie's Quilted Mysteries
Series Creator: Shari Lohner
Series Editors: Shari Lohner, Janice Tate, and Ken Tate
Cover Illustration © Summersea/Dreamstime.com

10 11 12 13 14 | Printed in China | 9 8 7 6 5 4

Take your needle, my child, and work at your pattern; it will come out a rose by and by. Life is like that—one stitch at a time taken patiently and the pattern will come out all right like the embroidery.

—Oliver Wendell Holmes Sr.

one

Emma Cotton stood before the majesty of the Eiffel Tower, marveling at the workmanship required to chisel a replica of the French landmark out of a huge block of ice right in the town square of cozy Mystic Harbor, Massachusetts. Twinkle lights reflecting off the ice gave the illusion of a Parisian cityscape.

"I'll be the first to admit Valentine's Day isn't exactly my favorite holiday, but each year I'm amazed at the sculptures created for the Melting Hearts Festival," she said, bending her head slightly to inhale the warm, sweet steam of the hot chocolate clutched between her hands. "Look at the detail!"

A recording of *It Had to Be You* filtered softly through the chilly air as Emma and her friend and business partner, Kelly Grace, stepped closer to the sculpture to allow a couple and their two small giggling children to pass behind them.

"Each year it gets better and better," Kelly said, heading toward the next sculpture. "I don't know how they come up with so many different symbols of love. So far tonight we've seen storybook characters, animals, and dancers. What's next?"

"Fairies." Emma was frozen in place, her voice barely audible, staring at the ring of three fairies with long, flowing hair and delicate wings, their hands barely touching. "Rose loved fairies."

Kelly placed her gloved hand on Emma's arm and squeezed hard enough so the gesture was felt through the heavy coat sleeve. "Obsessed with them, actually. She never really outgrew her childhood fascination. I loved that about her," Kelly said.

"Me too." Emma's eyes fixed on the sculpture, but instead of three ice figures, she saw a trio of young girls—Rose with dark curly locks, Kelly with auburn-brown tresses, and the fair-headed Emma—holding hands as they skipped round and round in a fairy dance.

"Kelly, I've been thinking about Vanessa Nelson," she said, turning her gaze from the whimsical sculpture to look her friend in the eyes. "I think I've found a way—"

"No talk of murder suspects allowed today. We're here to relax a little, satisfy my chocolate cravings in every way possible, and enjoy the sculptures." Kelly gave Emma her best disciplinarian look, a skill honed when her two college-age children were little, and nudged her away from the fairies. "We agreed to keep a healthy balance between our lives and the investigation, remember?"

"Whatever do you mean? I have perfect balance—*ahhh!*" Hitting an icy patch of sidewalk, Emma's legs flew out from under her. Sliding down the slight incline, she landed at the feet of Cupid, his bow and arrow poised and ready to strike an unsuspecting target. The hot chocolate cup rolled to a stop next to her, its contents soaking her wrists and jacket.

Stunned, Emma watched as everyone around her began to spring into action. Kelly picked up Emma's shoulder bag—it had fallen off her shoulder by the fence surrounding Cupid—and held onto it while her friend collected her wits.

Martha Wood, the festival coordinator and president of the downtown merchants association, waddled over as quickly as her plump legs would allow. She was putting her cellphone in a jacket pocket as she walked up to Emma. "Don't move! I called Dr. Hart. He's on his way."

"I don't think that's necessary," Emma said, gingerly straightening her legs. "I'm fine. If you'll give me a hand—"

"Don't be silly." Martha, one hand on her hip and the other clutching a clipboard, looked down at Emma with the look of a stern army nurse. "We have to make sure you're all right and I must complete this incident form for insurance purposes. Rules are rules."

Kelly cleared her throat. "Don't look now, here comes Dr. Dreamy himself. Your aunt is going to love this!"

Emma glared at her. "You leave Dottie Faye out of this. If she finds out, I'll never live this down."

Emma's harsh words created a twinge of guilt. Aunt Dottie Faye would be concerned about Emma's fall, no matter how minor. Since arriving in Mystic Harbor after Emma's mom, Dottie Faye's sister, died over two years ago, Dottie Faye, while more than a bit eccentric, had been a comfort and kept life interesting.

Much to Emma's constant irritation, Dottie Faye was a perennial matchmaker and had her sights set on Dr. Eric Hart for her niece. Nothing would make her aunt happier than to see her married to a doctor with a Southern heritage. Thank goodness she was minding Emma and Kelly's shop, Cotton & Grace quilt designs. She needn't know a thing about Dr. Hart's involvement. The last thing Emma wanted right now was her aunt's matchmaking.

Looking like a lumberjack in his red-and-black flannel jacket and blue jeans, Dr. Hart and his ten-year-old daughter, Riley, pushed through the gathering crowd.

He knelt down and grinned as he unzipped Emma's boots and checked to make sure her ankles weren't swollen. "I see you're getting a bit up close and personal with Cupid here. This ground is cold. Let's get you to the first-aid tent. It's warm in there."

Kelly snickered and grinned when Emma threw her a warning look. "I guess you could say Emma fell head over heels for Cupid!"

Jumping to her feet in hopes of making a hasty retreat from the romantic ribbing, Emma took a tentative step but immediately sat back down when pain soared from her right ankle. "Maybe I'll sit a bit longer."

Before she could protest, Eric pulled her to her feet without skipping a beat, scooped her into his arms, and took long strides down the pathway toward the tent. "Relax and enjoy the ride. The tent is just on the other side of the square," he said.

Emma glowered, her face tinged in crimson. Attempting to avoid eye contact, Emma glanced down to find Riley walking beside them. "I'm sorry I interrupted your outing with your dad, Riley."

The girl shrugged. "That's OK. I think he likes playing the knight in shining armor. We were almost finished looking at the sculptures anyway."

Eric cleared his throat. "Riley, Miss Cotton spilled her hot chocolate when she fell. Would you please go buy her another one? I'll stop by and pay for it later." Emma squirmed in protest, which only resulted in the doctor tightening his arms around her. "It's OK. Consider it part of the personalized care I extend to all my patients."

Kelly looked longingly at the chocolate booth. "I think I'll tag along with Riley. All the excitement has stirred up my chocolate craving. I'll find something positively decadent to take our minds off your fall."

Emma watched helplessly as Kelly disappeared into the crowd before taking a quick peek at Eric's face. She had to admit, he was handsome with his light blond hair and brown eyes. It was probably safer to not look into his eyes. An awkward silence fell between them as Eric carried her through the crowd. A sigh of relief escaped her when he finally eased her into a chair inside the first-aid tent.

Eric knelt beside her, his eyes darkened with concern. "Did I hurt your ankle when I put you down?"

"Not at all. I'm relieved to be sitting still for a moment. I probably could have walked here myself. You didn't need to go to all this trouble."

When Kelly and Riley returned with hot chocolate and enough confections to satisfy the worst sweet tooth, Eric was satisfied there were no broken bones and was putting first-aid cream on the spot where the hot cocoa had spilled on Emma's wrist.

"It's a good thing your shop is close by. I suggest you take it easy for the remainder of the day and rest your ankle frequently over the weekend. Be careful of hidden ice." His eyes twinkled with amusement. "And beware of Cupid's aim."

Emma stood to leave, thanked Eric for his time and the hot cocoa Riley had brought her, and was about to hobble out of the tent when she heard her name barked from the door of the tent.

"Oh no you don't. You can't leave until you and the doctor sign this release form. We have rules, you know." Martha held out the clipboard and blocked the door until Emma had scribbled her name by the red X on the form.

As Martha snatched the clipboard from Emma's hand, Kelly locked her arm through Emma's and eased her out of the tent. "I'd like to tell her what to do with those rules," Kelly whispered as the tent flap closed behind them. She held a paper bag out to Emma. "Here, have a chocolate delight bar. It's guaranteed to cure what ails you."

Not one to overindulge in sweets, Emma hesitated before

fishing the last bar out of the bag. Her stomach growled. The gooey treat tasted sinful, and Emma realized she was ravenous after the excitement of the afternoon. "Wow, this is incredible. It really is delightful."

Kelly squeezed Emma's arm and chuckled. "What was incredible was the way Eric looked at you with those dreamy eyes of his. You know, I think falling at Cupid's feet was a good omen."

"Oh no! *Et tu, Brute?*" said Emma, doing her best Julius Caesar imitation. "Stupid Cupid. Anyway, I don't believe in omens."

Aunt Dottie Faye Sinclair, who publicly denied being old enough to be Emma's mother's sister, was waiting at the door of Cotton & Grace when the two shop owners crossed Gallows Way.

"Emma Jane. Why are you limping?" Dottie Faye's Southern accent was particularly thick when heightened emotion was involved. She opened the door wider, allowing Emma and Kelly to enter at the same time. As soon as they were through, Dottie Faye let it slam behind them so she could grab Emma's other arm and help lead her to the comfy chairs in the design area.

Emma's aunt patted the seat cushion. "Sit here, child, and tell me all about it. I want to hear every single detail."

"Boy, do we have some details for you, Dottie Faye." Kelly said, drawing a frown from Emma.

Emma tried to tell an abridged version of the story by leaving out the statue of Cupid and the part about being carried away by Eric Hart. She knew this information would encourage Dottie Faye to refer to him as Prince Charming or some such nonsense. But Kelly filled in these details with glee.

"Honestly, if it wasn't for Kelly Ann, I would never hear all the juicy details of your life," Dottie Faye chided before her candy-apple–red lips curled into a sly grin. "Dr. Eric is such a gentleman of fine Southern stock. He's handsome too."

Kelly glanced at the grandfather clock, disappeared into the stockroom, and returned with an old straight-back chair so Emma could prop up her foot. "You sit right here and rest. I'll close up shop. Don't even try to get up, or I'll sic Dottie Faye on you."

"And I," said Dottie Faye, shaking a long, bright red fingernail under Emma's nose, "will call Dr. Eric in a heartbeat if you so much as attempt to stand on that ankle."

Feeling a bit tired and achy from the fall, Emma leaned back in the chair and let them have their way, at least temporarily. They couldn't keep her down for long. "Honestly, you two are like a pair of mother hens."

"Well, someone must take care of you since you don't seem to be in any hurry to find a man to do it." Dottie Faye turned her attention to packing up the remainder of the chocolate-dipped strawberries, white-chocolate–coated pretzels, and sparkling punch from the refreshment table. "I love Valentine's Day. It's so romantic. Maybe you were destined to slip by Cupid and land in the arms of Mystic Harbor's most eligible bachelor."

A chuckle filtered from behind the cash register where Kelly was shutting it down for the day. "Well, as close as Emma fell to that statue, I'd be surprised if Cupid's arrow didn't hit its mark."

Emma wasn't sure how many more Cupid comments she could take. "Dottie Faye, thanks so much for boxing up the goodies. Why don't you head on home now? You've been here nearly all day."

She was relieved when her aunt quickly agreed to leave because the Friday-night dance at the American Legion was getting ready to start. As soon as Dottie Faye had closed the door behind her, Emma rose from the chair and hobbled over to Kelly. "Would you *please* not encourage her? I'll never hear the end of this Cupid thing."

"*Moi?* What did I do?" Kelly's deep blue eyes sparkled with mischief.

Emma couldn't help but smile. She knew Kelly enjoyed egging on Dottie Faye and her outrageous notions. Her aunt had practically adopted Kelly as her own. "Are you about ready to go?"

Fifteen minutes later, the shop was locked up. Emma and Kelly, arm in arm, stepped off the curb to cross Gallows Way to their cars. The festivities over, the street was quiet and filled with eerie shadows cast by the old-fashioned streetlamps. Their breath sent silent clouds of mist into the air. Emma was glad they shared an easy friendship, one that didn't require constant chatter at the end of a busy day.

The peaceful night was pierced by a bone-chilling *kee-eeeee-arr* as a winged creature rose from a lamppost and darted over their heads. The two women watched in awe as the hawk screamed again before gaining altitude and disappearing into the darkness.

"Wow," Emma said, staring into the dark sky. "What's a hawk doing here in the middle of winter, after dark no less?

"I've never seen one come so close before." Kelly lightly nudged Emma's shoulder. "Maybe he was sending you some sort of message or asking you who was going to make the first move, you or Eric."

Stopping beside her Jeep, Emma turned to look Kelly in the eyes. "I don't have time for romance. Between the investigation into Rose's death, the shop, and all the volunteer activities Dottie Faye keeps dragging me into, my life is already full."

Kelly shook her head. "Emma, I saw the look on Eric's face when he lifted you into his arms. This could be the beginning of something special." Kelly paused and her eyes softened. "You've got to let the memory of Rose move over and allow some room in your heart. I don't mean you should forget her, even if you could. But you need to get out and experience life more. Rose would want that for you."

Pointing her key fob at the vehicle, Emma unlocked the door but paused and stared at Kelly. "I don't want to talk about this anymore."

two

Emma was usually one of the first to arrive at the quaint sewing and quilting shop, Uncommon Threads, each Saturday for the Nimble Thimbles meeting and a morning of communal quilting. She would meander among the bolts of colorful material in the renovated old Montgomery Ward building. While checking out new arrivals and chatting with the shop's owner, Marcia Goode, she'd often spy the perfect fabric for the creation of a computer case, diaper bag, craft tote, or other design before dashing up the creaky old stairs to the meeting.

But today she didn't wander the aisles. She was moving about as fast as a Ferrari stuck in deadlocked Boston rush-hour traffic.

Laughter echoed down the stairs as the Nimble Thimbles prepared to begin their weekly quilting meeting.

Emma placed her left foot on the bottom step of the wooden staircase, paused, and slowly lifted her other foot to rest beside it. She was a little stiff from yesterday's fall, but her ankle only hurt when she put her full weight on it. *One step at a time.*

"Emma Jane." Dottie Faye's voice was so close her breath tickled Emma's ear. "Why are you struggling when there's an able-bodied gentleman upstairs? And you know there is a perfectly good elevator to use, if you must."

Her aunt meant well, but Emma wasn't cut from the same cloth. After all, she'd been a New Englander since she was seven years old. Her voice didn't have a shred of Southern accent, and she hadn't been raised to be a helpless female. She didn't want a man to wait on her hand and foot. She didn't even want one underfoot.

"I'm perfectly fine. I don't need the elevator," Emma said, stifling a groan as she moved to the next step to prove her point.

"Perfectly stubborn is what you are." Dottie Faye squeezed in the narrow space beside Emma and grabbed her elbow. "Don't make a scene; let me help you."

To keep the peace, Emma swallowed her protestations and allowed Dottie Faye to accompany her up the stairs. With any luck, the ankle would be forgotten among other topics of conversation during the meeting.

She should have known better.

Dottie Faye announced their arrival as soon as she reached the top step.

"Here she is, all safe and sound." she said, leading Emma to the closest chair. "Our Emma has had quite the exciting weekend so far."

Emma felt all eyes turn to her. Luckily the group was small because many of the quilters were at the festival with their families. "Good morning. I'm sure everyone has more interesting topics to discuss than my ankle, which is fine, by the way. Aren't the ice sculptures incredible this year?"

Often the quilters spread out in the room, with one using the sewing machine, a few surrounding the worktable, a couple of others sitting at the quilting frames, and the rest nestled in several comfortable old chairs. But today everyone sat clustered around the table and seemed more eager to chat about the festival than to seriously work on quilting.

Tokala Abrams looked up from the earth-toned fabrics nestled on her lap, her dark eyes smiling above her high cheekbones. "I particularly enjoyed the inspiration the artists found in wild animals this year. They went beyond the usual swans and included jumping fish and a family of bears."

Emma watched Walter Russell pull a needle and thread through a corner of a square and tie it with arthritic fingers. She knew Valentine's Day was difficult for him since his wife died a few years ago. "Your quilt is really shaping up, Walter," she said. "It'll be done in plenty of time for your daughter's birthday."

He smiled and his face brightened. "Angie will be so surprised. She still can't believe her mathematician father enjoys something as creative as quilting." Walter smoothed the quilt and ran his fingers over the tulips and daisies, his daughter's favorite flowers. "She brought my granddaughter Caroline to the festival yesterday. Caroline loved the animals, but my favorite sculpture was of the old couple on the bench. It made me think of my wife."

The room was silent and Emma tried to think of something to say, words that wouldn't sound trite. Her friend Marcia Goode, leader of the Nimble Thimbles, popped in to check on the group.

"How's it going in here? I haven't abandoned you, I promise." Marcia said, a bit breathless from her sprint up the stairs. "I've been busy with festival visitors. We've had such a great turnout this year."

Her eyes scanned the room. "We're missing a couple of regulars. Where are Maeve and Kelly this morning?"

Emma shifted in her chair and repositioned her right foot. "They're at our shop, preparing refreshments and freebies for today. We are handing out bookmarks with quilting tips and Maeve's delectable chocolate Irish cream brownies—non-alcoholic, of course."

As if on cue, Kelly and her mother, Maeve Quigley, waltzed into the meeting area.

"Here we are, and we've brought brownies. Grab one before

Kelly does," Maeve announced, balancing the plate with one hand. "And we left a couple of customers downstairs."

Dottie Faye rolled her eyes and leaned over to Emma. "Leave it to that woman to make an entrance."

A chuckle escaped Emma's lips as she watched Marcia disappear down the stairs. Her aunt was notorious for attracting attention wherever she went. "Yeah, you have that pot-kettle thing down pat, Dottie Faye."

Launching into a fake cough, Dottie Faye reached down and put her quilt squares in the bag at her feet. "Anyway, as I was saying earlier, Emma Jane drew quite the attention yesterday when she was felled by Cupid's arrow and rescued by our own dreamy Dr. Hart. He took care of her ankle and even carried her to the first-aid tent."

Maeve set the plate of brownies on the edge of the worktable and took a seat next to Emma. "How are you feeling, Emma?"

"I'm fine, really. A bit stiff from the fall, but I'll survive."

"She'd be better if she'd give that young Dr. Hart a chance instead of acting so independent all the time." Dottie Faye grinned in triumph, having successfully regained control of the conversation. "Honestly, sugar, there are times when a Southern belle needs to be needy."

Emma looked up at the natural light streaming through the room's two huge windows. She wished she could climb the sunbeams and escape this conversation. Tokala came to the rescue.

"Emma, how's the investigation into your friend's death going? You've not mentioned it in a while."

Emma wasn't sure where to start. After fifteen years of haunted dreams, she and Kelly were finally making some headway in finding out why Rose had been killed in a fall down the stairs at Hawthorne College, but they had a long way to go. It had been a stroke of luck when Dottie Faye discovered the unattractive quilt Rose's mother had given Emma after the funeral, only to be tucked away in storage. Despite its crooked seams, mismatched designs, and clashing colors, the quilt held a long-sought treasure—the names of the students attending Rose's college class at the time she died. So far, they'd contacted and cleared four of the twelve students on the suspect list created from the names on the quilt.

Tokala was right; it had taken them too long to follow their latest lead. Nearly a month had passed since their trip to England to meet Rose's blue-blooded former student and castle owner, Colin Dudley, and they hadn't yet followed up on the tip he'd given them. They'd been too busy catching up on a quilt restoration project for the senator's wife and preparing for the Melting Hearts Festival to do much more than computer searches for information about the latest suspect, Vanessa Nelson.

"Now that the quilt for the senator's wife is finished and this festival is nearly behind us, we will finally have more time to chase down Vanessa Nelson," Emma said. "Colin—he's the innkeeper in England and one of the last to see Rose alive—said Vanessa was the student who made the quilt out of the squares created by all of Rose's students."

Snitching the first brownie, Kelly took a bite and nodded with satisfaction. "These are fantabulous. By the way, we discovered that Vanessa still lives nearby. She's the assistant curator at the Boston Fine Arts Museum. Emma is thrilled we don't have to board a transatlantic flight to find this suspect."

"I love that museum," said Walter. He glanced up from his stitching. "My wife and I spent a lot of time there. In fact, they have a new exhibit featuring an array of textiles from different time periods and countries. There's a reception on Thursday. It might be a good opportunity for you to talk to a lot of people and take a look around. Maybe meet this Vanessa."

Kelly plucked a tissue from the side pocket of her craft tote and wiped a crumb from her chin. "That's a great idea. Refreshments are usually really tasty at art receptions," she said, stuffing the tissue back in her bag. "We might even be able to get a DNA sample from a fork or napkin without needing to confront Vanessa and explain what we're doing."

Nodding, Emma considered Kelly's suggestion. So far they'd managed to collect DNA samples from four of the students who had attended Rose's class the night she died. One sample was a lucky find at Cotton & Grace after an arsonist had set fire to the shop; another was swiped from manicure scrapings; the third was on a bandage a suspect had peeled from her finger; and the last was on a linen napkin. A quick, albeit expensive, analysis by the private lab Genetix had ruled out each suspect.

"That's not a bad idea," Emma said. "We're getting pretty good at getting the samples. Eventually we'll find a match to one of the two skin scrapings found under Rose's fingernails. "

Dottie Faye clicked her own long, lacquered nails together and shook her head. "The museum director is a man, I believe," she said, batting her mascara-laden eyelashes. "I think you should let me go undercover and scope things out for you."

Maeve rolled her green eyes. "Doreen Hallinan is a volunteer there, a fine, hardworking woman. I can see what she knows about Vanessa. That might be more effective."

Emma and Kelly exchanged glances. Maeve and Dottie Faye were trying to outdo each other. This could get ugly. "Let us know what Doreen says, Mom," Kelly said.

The antique clock in the corner chimed ten times. The morning was fleeing, and Emma wasn't in the mood to watch another round of Dottie Faye versus Maeve. "Kelly, we really need to get to the shop. We probably have customers waiting on us."

Kelly snagged another brownie off the plate as she left the room. "Mom, would you please bring the dish back with you?"

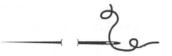

Emma and Kelly stuck to the main path across the town square and walked as quickly as Emma's ankle and the crowds would allow. They didn't want to keep potential customers waiting outside the shop.

"You were oddly quiet during the discussion about Vanessa and the museum, although I thought you were going to yank the silk rose from Dottie Faye's hair when she suggested using her feminine wiles on the museum director," Kelly said. "Why?"

Stopping to rest her ankle, Emma allowed a slow grin to cross her face. "Yesterday I emailed the volunteer coordinator about helping at the museum. We should hear something soon."

Kelly lightly slapped her friend's shoulder. "You sly dog. You didn't tell me."

Emma nodded, a smile tugging at the corners of her mouth. "I wanted it to be a surprise."

Crossing Gallows Way, they watched a trio of women peer into the door of Cotton & Grace. "Look, our public awaits." Kelly said, stepping up to the curb. "We're open." she called to the prospective customers. "We'll be right there."

The rest of the day passed in a blur of visitors singing the praises of Maeve's brownies, complimenting the bookmarks, requesting information about quilt restoration, and purchasing discounted items. The diaper bags and craft totes drew the most attention. Each time Emma tried to move around the shop to help a customer, Kelly shooed her back to the computer at the checkout counter and told her to rest her ankle.

The sun had already set by the time Emma and Kelly began closing up the shop. Emma checked her email one last time. "Kelly, do you suppose Maeve can watch the shop on Monday? You and I have volunteer training at the museum most of the day."

Vanessa Nelson certainly wasn't what Emma had expected.

The statuesque blonde in stilettos oozed boredom as she surveyed the classroom and extended a half-hearted handshake when the volunteer coordinator, Helene Floros, first introduced Emma and Kelly. This was the woman who had thought enough of Rose to make a keepsake quilt for her?

Vanessa perked up a bit when Helene mentioned that Emma and Kelly were in the quilt design and restoration business.

"Cotton & Grace? Yes, I am familiar with your work, although I've not been in your shop for quite some time. What made you decide to volunteer at the museum?" Vanessa tugged the sleeve of her burgundy silk blouse until it peeked out of the jacket cuff. She tossed her head and glanced at the clock on the wall, which read nine fifty-five.

What made her ask that? Could she possibly know why they were there? Emma looked into Vanessa's green-blue eyes for a clue. She saw nothing, not even a smidge of warmth.

"We're always looking for ways to give back to the community," Emma answered. "With our line of work, the art museum seemed like a natural fit."

Kelly swallowed the last bite of cookie she had grabbed

from the refreshment table and wiped her mouth with a napkin. "My mom knows Doreen Hallinan. Doreen has been singing the museum's praises for years."

After glancing at the clock again, Vanessa nodded. "We're about ready to start."

Kelly and Emma watched her walk to the front of the room and stand next to a man they assumed was Gabe Lucier, the museum's executive director. Tall, broad shouldered, and sporting a short and neatly trimmed beard, he looked more like a well-dressed linebacker than a museum director.

"Wow. Do you suppose there's ice running through those veins?" Kelly said a bit more loudly than Emma would have preferred.

"It seems possible," said Emma before leading Kelly to a seat near the back of the room in order to observe the others.

As various museum staffers were introduced, Emma noted their titles and job duties. She also watched Vanessa's body language and interaction with her colleagues, jotting coded comments in her volunteer manual. Vanessa seemed knowledgeable about the museum and its collections. She was professional, but aloof.

Kelly studied the map of the museum, noting the location of Vanessa's office and other areas to explore during the break. After a couple of hours, she began fidgeting so much that Emma reached over and placed her hand on Kelly's arm. "Hang in there, Kelly, we should have a break soon."

Kelly pushed her copy of the map closer to Emma and pointed to an office located on the same floor as the classrooms. Tapping her finger on a small rectangle she had labeled "V.O.," she mouthed, "Vanessa's office."

Emma nodded and traced a route to the office with her finger. It wouldn't be too difficult to find. Engrossed in her thoughts, she was startled when Helene announced lunch. As soon as the volunteer coordinator finished giving instructions, Emma jumped out of her chair and turned toward the door. "Come on, let's go."

"Emma, it won't hurt to grab a sandwich first and maybe a couple of cookies. I'm starving." Kelly looked longingly at the spread of boxed lunches and canned drinks waiting at the back of the room.

"We'll have time to eat later. We need to find the restroom," said Emma, grabbing the sleeve of Kelly's sweater.

"But I don't need to—" Kelly's words were cut short by Emma's glare. "Oh, OK. Follow me. I have the map."

They found Vanessa's office on the other end of the horse-shoe of hallways on the third floor. Their footsteps seemed deafening in the silence.

"Here it is." Emma tapped on the door. Getting no response, she tried the doorknob. It was locked.

Kelly rummaged around in her purse. "I think I have Dottie Faye's lock-picking tools in here somewhere. Ahhh, here they—"

A cold, shrill voice behind them cut the silence. "Just what do you two think you're doing?"

three

Kelly jumped and nearly dropped the pouch of tools as Vanessa's voice sliced through the quiet hallway. "We were looking for a restroom. But we saw your name on the door—"

"One of the volunteers told us to be sure to see the fiber art in your office. She said it was of rare quality," Emma interjected, dropping her hand from the doorknob and stepping out of Vanessa's way.

Vanessa glanced at her watch before stepping past Emma and unlocking the office door. "Well, the restrooms are located a few doors down from the classroom where we were, so you walked right past them."

Emma saw their chance to collect a DNA sample slipping away.

"We'd really love to see your fiber art pieces, since we're here. We won't take much of your time." Emma pulled a business card from the side pocket of her shoulder bag and handed it to Vanessa. "We're always looking to experience something new."

Silence hung in the air. Vanessa slowly nodded as she pushed on the door and held it open as Emma and Kelly walked into the room.

The first piece of fiber art they saw stopped them in their tracks.

"Vanessa, that is so Rose—" Emma began.

Kelly cleared her throat. "What she means is it is crazy

creative how you took inspiration from art nouveau–style roses but made them contemporary. I've not seen anything quite like it."

Vanessa smiled what Emma thought was her first genuine expression since they had met that morning. "Thank you. This piece means a lot to me."

"I can see why," said Emma, still gazing at the bright, circular roses with their spiny 3-D thorns. "It's so whimsical yet bold. It feels good."

"It was inspired by the young woman who taught me the fundamentals of quilt design." Vanessa's face softened. "She was a gifted instructor and doctoral candidate at Hawthorne College. Her passion for fiber art was contagious."

Emma pressed one hand over her chest with the other as if this would slow the pounding of her heart. "She must be very proud of you. Have you kept in touch with her?"

"Unfortunately, she died shortly after our last class." Vanessa turned toward the opposite wall and motioned toward another quilt. "I completed this one while finishing my own doctoral studies at Massachusetts College of Art and Design."

Emma could have sworn she'd heard the ice queen's voice catch when the subject of Rose's death had come up. She wasn't sure her own voice could be trusted. She glanced at Kelly, who responded with a slight nod.

"It's equally gorgeous," Kelly said. "What was your inspiration for this one? It's so very different."

Before Vanessa could answer, Gabe Lucier appeared in the doorway and motioned Vanessa into the hallway. "May I see you in my office?" he asked. "I have questions about the abstract expressionism exhibit." He smiled at Emma and Kelly. "She'll just be a few minutes."

"Certainly." Vanessa looked at Emma and Kelly. "Feel free

to look at the fiber art books on the shelf. I think you'll find them interesting."

When the door closed behind Vanessa, Emma leapt behind the desk and opened the bottom left drawer. "What luck! You take the right side. Maybe we can find a coffee cup or something in here to get a DNA sample from."

They rummaged through the desk drawers in silence until Kelly pumped her fist in triumph. "Yes! Here's a hairbrush. It looks like there are some roots attached to the hair. Hand me a sample bag."

As Kelly started to snatch the bag from Emma's fingers, the sound of the doorknob turning startled them. Kelly shoved the drawer shut with her hip and turned to face the large antique tapestry hanging behind Vanessa's desk. "How old do you suppose this is, Emma?"

"About a hundred and fifty years," said Vanessa. "Why are you behind my desk? You can see it better from back here."

Emma leaned closer to the tapestry. "I wanted to see the detail." The clock's ticking seemed louder as she moved toward the door. "Thank you for showing us your quilts. I guess we should get back to orientation."

"Don't forget—you'll find the restroom on the way," Vanessa said, the ice returning to her voice.

Emma's feeling of frustration at missing an opportunity to get Vanessa's DNA turned to surprise as she and Kelly walked in the door of Cotton & Grace. Dottie Faye and Maeve were huddled in the alcove and seemed deep in conversation—civil conversation instead of their normal verbal sparring.

Emma looked at Kelly, blinked, and glanced around the room, looking for evidence of bloodshed or broken objects. Everything was in perfect order; even Bach's Brandenburg Concerto No. 3 was playing softly on the sound system. Emma felt like she was in the middle of an episode of *The Twilight Zone*.

"Who are you and what have you done with Dottie Faye and Maeve?"

Dottie Faye jumped, looking like she had been caught kissing her best friend's sweetheart. The large pink orbs dangling from her ears swayed as she looked down to make sure her deep purple sweater was pulled down evenly over her black leggings. "Oh, sugar pie, you do have the most bizarre sense of humor."

Hands on her hips, Kelly looked from her mother to Dottie Faye. "What are you two doing?"

Maeve walked across the shop and grabbed her bag from behind the counter. After a quick glance at Dottie Faye, she reached in and pulled out an envelope. "Just killing time waiting for Emma." She held the packet, a smile curling her lips. "I stopped by to give you these two tickets so you and Dottie Faye can attend the hospital's Heart of Hearts Ball. I thought you'd enjoy a night out."

Emma took the envelope and removed the tickets. "Two weeks from Saturday. Thank you, but I think Kelly and Patrick might make better use of these."

"Nonsense," said Dottie Faye before Maeve could take a breath. "We will have a fabulous time. And you need to get out more. This is your chance."

Tapping Emma on the shoulder, Kelly broke into a giggle. "I think you're double-teamed here. You may want to give in on this one. Anyway, it wouldn't hurt you to go out and hear some good music and eat scrumptious food. Give in this time."

"If I agree to go, will all of you stop harassing me about my social life? At least for a little while?"

"Yes, we sure will," said Maeve. "Besides, we have more important things to discuss, like when you will begin pulling out the St. Patrick's Day decorations."

"Oh no you don't." Dottie Faye clutched to her chest a heart-shaped pillow with Cupid and the phrase "Love is all we need" cross-stitched on it. "You can't rush the holiday of romance and love."

"Sure we can," said Emma, casting a thankful look to Maeve. "St. Patrick's Day is important to Maeve and Kelly. It won't hurt to have the Celtic decorations ready to roll when the time comes." She cast an invitation of solidarity to Kelly. It was ignored. Obviously Kelly was enjoying the verbal volley.

"Emma Jane, how could you choose *her* holiday over the day of *looove*? Honestly!" Dottie Faye's Southern accent had become even more pronounced.

The voice of reason came from Maeve.

"Well, I can't discount the power of love. Cupid can work magic on the heart." Maeve twisted the ring she still wore on her left hand although her husband had been gone for ten years. "I still miss Sean."

"Amen to that." Dottie Faye jumped to her stiletto-clad feet and tossed the pillow onto the chair. "Now, tell us all about your volunteer orientation."

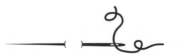

Emma tapped her foot as she gazed into her closet, looking for something suitable to wear to the ball. She had sensible skirts, blouses, and jackets for work and a few dresses she wore to church. Plenty of slacks and sweaters. A smattering of nice shoes. No formal wear.

She sat on the bed. Fatigue and frustration washed over her. It had been a long day, and she wasn't any closer to knowing if Vanessa had been involved in Rose's death than she had been that morning. A whole day wasted. She had no DNA from Vanessa, no desire for romance, and no dress for the ball.

"I don't have anything to wear," she said. "There's no way I can go to the ball."

"Now that is the silliest thing I've ever heard you say." Dottie Faye's words drowned out the words in her head and catapulted Emma to her feet.

"Dottie Faye." Emma backed into her dresser and sagged against it. "How many times do I need to tell you to stop sneaking up on me?"

Her aunt tossed a blue garment bag and a shoebox onto the bed. "What's all this about not going to the ball? Now you have the perfect gown and the perfect shoes. I know because I picked them out myself."

Emma stared at the bag and hoped the dress inside it was not bright pink with the feathers and sequins her aunt was fond of wearing. "You shouldn't have, really."

"Oh, posh." Dottie Faye waved away Emma's protest, the glitter on her nails catching the lamplight. "What good is my money if I can't spend it on my favorite niece? Now, open the bag."

Emma slowly tugged on the zipper and caught her breath as she exposed the dress, the long version of a little black one—long sleeves, classic V-neck, with silver embroidery on the fitted waistband. "Oh, Dottie Faye, this is … stunning. It is too much."

"Look at the shoes." Dottie Faye's eyes sparkled as much

as her fingernails as Emma lifted the shoebox lid and pulled out a sleek black pump with a hint of silver stitching on the toe.

Dottie Faye had outdone herself. Emma wasn't quite sure what to say. She couldn't have chosen a more perfect outfit if she had handpicked it personally. But going to a ball wasn't exactly her idea of a fantastic time. "This is really important to you—going to this ball—isn't it?"

Grabbing Emma's hands in her own, Dottie Faye led her to the bench at the foot of the bed.

"Emma Jane, I'm worried that you're getting stressed out between the demands of the shop, investigating Rose's murder, and now you're adding volunteer work at the museum." Dottie Faye squeezed Emma's hands. "I want you to have a little fun. And you need to get out more. You haven't dated anyone since your breakup with Josh."

"Dottie Faye, I'm really OK. But I love you for caring." Emma removed her hands from Dottie Faye's grasp. "I must admit I'll feel better once we find out who killed Rose."

"We'll find out what happened on that dreadful night," said Dottie Faye, her voice softening. "But in the meantime, you need to live your life. It's what Rose would want."

Emma stifled a yawn and nodded. "Yes, we will find out. I won't stop searching until we do. But right now, I need to get some sleep. It's been a busy day."

She walked Dottie Faye to the front door and gave her a hug. "Thank you for the dress and for being here."

"I'll always be here, sugar. Don't you ever forget it," Dottie Faye said, nudging Emma's nose before walking out the door and closing it behind her.

Emma bolted the front door and snapped off the lights before heading down the hallway to her room. The ball gown was spread across the bed, the shoes nestled in their open box. She definitely had to attend the ball now.

Fifteen minutes later, after completing her nightly bedtime routine, Emma slipped underneath her quilt and melted into the mattress. Sleep was swift. And so was the dream.

Clad in a black formal gown and glittering high heels, Emma stumbled through her dream world, endlessly searching the echoing, ever-expanding hallways of Hawthorne College for Rose. The distant whirl of her breath filled her ears as she raced time and a faceless killer. Surely she was getting closer. Where were they? Why couldn't she hear Rose screaming? Screams would lead her to Rose. Her breathing slowed. A hawk darted down the hallway and flew by her head, filling the air with a bone-chilling, piercing cry.

"Rose." Emma sat up, her heart thumping against her chest. Fighting her way out of a sleepy fog, she shook her head to clear her mind. The hawk was new. What did it mean?

four

"I've always loved this building," Kelly said as Emma pulled the Jeep into the volunteer parking area of the Boston Fine Arts Museum. "Remember the summer when Rose's mom signed us all up for art lessons? How old were we, twelve?"

Emma chuckled at the memory. The imposing gray brick building with its castlelike towers and pointed arches would look right at home if plunked down in the middle of a fairy-tale land, especially with the morning sun casting a warm glow on its walls. "How could I forget? Before the first session ended, Rose had turned the three of us into princesses and the museum into an enchanted castle. One minute we were fairies, and the next we were royalty."

"Maybe you'll do Rose proud Saturday night and find yourself a Prince Charming," Kelly said. "It could happen, especially with the new threads Dottie Faye gave you."

"Kelly, you have an overactive imagination. The country club is nothing like an enchanted castle, and Prince Charming isn't likely to show up at a boring fundraiser. So, could we please concentrate on Vanessa?"

"Sure thing, Captain, Sir," said Kelly, stiffening into a dramatic salute.

Laughing, they crossed the parking lot and found a small crowd of people waiting outside the side entrance.

"Here I was afraid I was running late and they've not even opened the door yet," Kelly said as they found a spot on the edge of the group.

The gray-haired woman standing next to her turned and smiled. "Actually, the volunteer coordinator came out a few minutes ago and explained they were taking care of a personnel issue, but we'd be allowed into the building shortly." Her breath sent little puffs of vapor into the cool air. Emma remembered her from the volunteer training. She'd been interested in grant writing.

Emma leaned closer to Kelly, lips close to her ear. "I hope it's very shortly. The sooner we get Vanessa's DNA sample, the quicker we can get back to the shop."

"It had better be soon. I left my gloves in the car," said Kelly, rubbing her hands together before jamming them into her coat pockets.

The volunteers' conversation halted as the door opened and the security guard led a glaring Vanessa to a car in the employee parking lot. "This is absolutely ludicrous," she said, pointing her key fob at a beige Toyota Camry. The grim-faced but boyish-looking guard stood nearby as she slid behind the steering wheel, started her car, and squealed out of the parking lot. When she had disappeared down the street, he ambled back to the building.

"We're sorry you had to start your day witnessing that," he said, unlocking the museum door. He smiled easily and seemed to put the incident behind him. "Welcome to those of you who are new volunteers. I'm Jake Allen. I'll be at this door each day when you arrive for your shift. Once I check your names, you are free to report to your posts."

After checking in, they walked through the side lobby in search of Helene Floros. "He was kinda cute, in a rugged sort of way. Enough lines on his face to give him character, but a thick head of hair to run fingers through," Kelly said, giving Emma a nudge. "Don't you think?"

"Honestly, I didn't notice. I'm more interested in finding out why our latest suspect was led out of the building by a security guard. How in the world we are going to get a DNA sample now?"

Footsteps reverberated between the polished floors and walls of the nearly deserted museum as they walked across the tiles. It wouldn't be open to the public for another hour.

Helene, whose Greek heritage gave her face a healthy glow even in the dead of winter, was waiting for them across the side entrance lobby and standing inside the alcove housing a single elevator. "Good morning. Welcome to your first day as museum volunteers."

"We're happy to be here. Our history at this museum goes back a long way, since we took art classes here as kids," Kelly said, her eyes roaming the walls lined with the museum's permanent collection. "By the way, what was all the excitement in the parking lot?"

Helene leaned toward them, brushed a wisp of fine gray hair from her eyes, and lowered her voice. "A valuable painting is missing, and the museum director has reason to believe our assistant curator, Vanessa Nelson, knows something about it."

The security guard and Gabe Lucier stood by the door, talking in low voices. Emma was torn between the desire to eavesdrop on their conversation and the chance to get more out of Helene. Could Vanessa be a murderer *and* a thief?

"What makes them think she is connected to the painting's disappearance?" Emma asked, trying to sound casual.

Helene glanced across the lobby at Mr. Lucier, cleared her throat, and handed a sheet of paper to each of them. "These are your volunteer areas and related duties. Emma, you're in the administrative offices on the third floor. Kelly, you've been assigned to the gift shop. Both of you are scheduled for the morning shift each Monday, so you can get back to your shop after lunchtime."

The elevator doors opened and out stepped a petite woman whose straight black hair hung to her waist despite the barrette clinching it at the nape of her neck. She walked up to the three women and held out her hand. "I'm Marta Singh-Moon, the public relations director. Welcome to the Boston Fine Arts Museum," she said. "Emma, I'll take you upstairs to your work space."

"This is my friend Kelly Grace," Emma said, nodding toward Kelly. "She's volunteering in the gift shop."

After shaking hands and exchanging pleasantries, Kelly followed Helene to the gift shop while Emma and Marta waited for the elevator. Marta explained the lay of the land. The public relations department shared a suite of offices with the personnel department on the third floor. Emma's work space would be in the suite.

Exiting the elevator, Emma realized she had been so preoccupied with Vanessa during the volunteer training that she hadn't taken time to appreciate the new wing of the museum. Her eyes roamed as she walked the sunny hallways. The museum board had done a fantastic job of blending the contemporary annex housing the classrooms and offices with the neoclassical architecture of the original building. The sleek design had a fairy-tale charm of its own, with light pouring in from the glass panes in the center of the ceiling and large windows forming the wall opposite the elevator. The only art here was in the lines of the building and the shadows formed by sun and steel.

Emma and Marta walked past the meeting room where the volunteer orientation had been held and turned down the hallway in which she and Kelly had found Vanessa's office. The administrative suite was located in the same hall. Maybe she could slip out and take a peek during break time.

Continuing the open, airy design, the administrative suite held only three areas enclosed with walls and doors—a conference room and offices for the personnel and public relations directors. The rest of the suite consisted of work spaces designed to foster conversation and communication. Emma's desk was right in the middle of them. She hoped this would lead to some productive eavesdropping. Maybe she could learn more about Vanessa.

Emma had been given the task of updating the museum's contact database, an easy but time-consuming job. The computer program was user-friendly, and soon she was working her way through the list faster than she had expected. She was surprised when Marta stopped by two hours later to see if she had any questions and to remind Emma to help herself to a cup of coffee at any time.

"Actually, coffee sounds really good, thanks. I think I'll freshen up in the ladies room and grab a cup on my way back." Emma stretched and then reached for her purse as she stood.

"I'll be in a meeting with Kayla Turner, the museum's curator, for about thirty minutes or so. If you need anything after that, please feel free to ask." Marta smiled and turned toward the door.

Shortly after Marta left for her meeting, Emma entered the hallway. But instead of turning right to go to the restrooms, she turned left and sauntered in the direction of Vanessa's office, rubber gloves and specimen bags ready to be used with speed and efficiency. She groaned when she stopped in front of the office. She'd missed her chance to get Vanessa's DNA. The door was sealed with yellow-and-black caution tape.

"Vanessa might have been nice enough at one time to have admired our Rose, but the girls in the gift shop certainly had mixed reviews," Kelly told Emma while stirring the ice in her soda.

Emma leaned forward so they could talk without yelling in the crowded Picture Perfect Café. They'd stopped for lunch a block away from the museum to satisfy Kelly's ever-complaining belly and to share information they had learned about Vanessa before heading to Cotton & Grace. They needed to be able to concentrate on shop business when they returned to the shop. "How so? Vanessa is a cold fish, that's for sure, although she was certainly seething while the security guy escorted her out of the building."

The conversation stopped as a blue jeans–clad server slid a cheeseburger with the works in front of Kelly and placed a bowl of potato soup and a chicken salad sandwich at Emma's place. "Is there anything else I can get for you?" A wisp of brown hair fell out of her ponytail, and she swatted it with the back of her hand.

Emma resisted the urge to say, "Yes, I'd like an order of DNA from a possible felon, please." Instead she said, "No, thank you. This looks good." As soon as she turned away, Emma resumed the conversation about Vanessa.

"So, what did you find out in the gift shop?"

"Well, Cammie Smythe said Vanessa seems to be a very good curator, but she is also pretty loose lipped and known to repeat secrets told to her in confidence. The gift shop girls tried to steer clear of her whenever possible."

"So, she's not exactly Rebecca of Sunnybrook Farm, but just

because she gossips doesn't mean she's a thief or cold-blooded killer." Emma let a spoonful of the thick, hot soup slide down her throat and warm her. "Oh wow. This is almost as good as your mom's potato soup."

"I'll do you a favor and keep that comment between us. Mom would have your hide if she heard you compare a restaurant soup favorably to hers."

"I appreciate that from the bottom of my heart. I'd like to live long enough to see your children make you a grandmother," said Emma, pausing to remove the top slice of bread from the sandwich and evenly redistribute the chicken salad before replacing it. "Anyway, back to Vanessa. The coffeepot and snacks are just outside Marta's office. As I was adding cream to my coffee, I overheard Marta and her secretary talking about Vanessa. Evidently, she had not been fired, but was placed on administrative leave until the painting is recovered, the crime solved, and Vanessa is either exonerated or charged."

Kelly put the burger on her plate and wiped her mouth with a napkin. "You know, from what I heard, most of the volunteers don't understand why Vanessa is the suspect in the theft in the first place." Kelly dragged a french fry through a blob of ketchup and popped it into her mouth.

"I can answer that," Emma said. "Marta told the development director that a painting value estimate sheet for the painting had been found on Vanessa's desk. That does make her seem guilty, doesn't it? I sure would like to know why Vanessa wasn't arrested."

Emma pushed her plate away. They needed to get back to Cotton & Grace so Dottie Faye could get ready for a social engagement. But they were returning empty-handed. How in the world would they find Vanessa in a city as large as

Boston? "We aren't any closer to getting Vanessa's DNA than we were this morning."

"Well, it's not quite that bad," Kelly said, pulling a piece of paper from her purse. "I found Vanessa's address on the gift shop's contact list."

five

Emma clenched both ends of the borrowed silver fox fur wrap with one hand and gripped the dashboard with the other as Dottie Faye's white Caddy slid to a halt in front of the Mystic Harbor Country Club. If the six-foot skid mark hadn't attracted everyone's attention, Emma was sure the stereo blaring the voice of Hank Williams Jr. asserting that "all my rowdy friends are comin' over tonight" had done the trick.

Dottie Faye removed chewing gum from her mouth and put it in the ashtray. "Sugar pie, there's no sense at all in putting in an appearance at the social event of the season if you don't make a grand entrance."

"I see," said Emma as she reached for her beaded black clutch purse. "And that's why you're wearing a leopard print halter dress in February?"

Her aunt grinned. "You got it. Just follow my—"

Dottie Faye's instructions were cut off when the valet parking attendants opened both front doors. It was obvious the young man on the driver's side was struggling to maintain his composure as Dottie Faye stuck one leg out of the car and her dress split to midthigh. "Take good care of my Caddy, and there will be a nice fat tip for you later," she said to him.

Emma, unaccustomed to walking in high heels and a narrow ball gown, struggled to keep up with Dottie Faye as they entered the ballroom until her aunt suddenly stopped at the threshold of a tropical wonderland.

"Oh, Dottie Faye, this is like another world." Couples danced among live trees—magnolias, azaleas, hibiscus, dogwood—decked with bright silk blossoms and twinkle lights. A faux full moon shone down from a starlit sky. The hospital had certainly gone all out with the decorations.

"Nothing says love like flowers, Emma Jane." Dottie Faye plucked a red hibiscus bloom from the trellis and tucked it behind her left ear. "Now, I want you to find the man of your dreams while I go introduce myself to that positively dreamy hunk standing by the magnolia tree over there."

"I'll be fine, Dottie Faye. You go knock 'em dead. I'm going to check out the buffet table." Emma gave her aunt a hug. "I'll catch up with you later."

She watched Dottie Faye strut to the magnolia and work her Southern charm on a considerably younger and not unattractive man. Her aunt's feminine wiles never ceased to amaze her.

When Emma's eyes had fully adjusted to the dim lighting, she decided to make her way to the hors d'oeuvre table located just past the bar between two weeping willow trees. She was halfway there when she froze, unable to believe the scene unfolding ahead of her.

Vanessa Nelson stood a few feet away, champagne glass in hand, engulfed in a heated argument with a striking bald man. Emma focused on the champagne flute Vanessa kept waving in his face. A DNA sample. She rubbed her fingers across her sequined clutch purse. No way was a glass going to fit in there. She didn't even have a tissue large enough to cover the entire glass. Maybe a handful of napkins would do.

Taking care to stay hidden from Vanessa, Emma squeezed through the crowd until she made it close enough to the hors d'oeuvre table to grab a handful of napkins. She tucked them into her purse but left it unzipped for easy access. She wondered what would happen if the event chairman caught her in the act of swiping a wad of cocktail napkins. But it was for a good cause, right?

Emma was struggling to get past a couple making goo-goo eyes at each other when Vanessa suddenly tossed the contents of her glass into her adversary's reddening face, deposited the flute on a nearby table, and disappeared into the crowd. Emma sprang into action, murmuring, "Excuse me," as she elbowed her way past the bald man toward the table. She was within arm's reach of the glass when she heard someone calling her name. Feeling a hand on her shoulder, she glanced to her right and found a smiling auburn-haired man about her age, who had probably been an athlete in his youth. Something about him looked familiar, but Emma couldn't quite place his face.

"Yes?" Emma searched her brain, trying to determine whether or not she should know his name. "I'm Emma. And you are?"

"Kelly's cousin, Aidan, although I didn't expect you to recognize me. I don't think you've seen me since the time I put the salamander down your back when we were kids about, what, thirty years ago?"

Maneuvering her position so she could keep an eye on Vanessa's glass, Emma shook his hand and guided him out of her field of view. "Yes, how could I miss the red hair? It's good to see you."

"You look great. When Aunt Maeve surprised me with tickets to the ball, she told me to look for you. I'm glad she did."

"Me too," Emma said, distracted by the fleeting opportunity to nab Vanessa's DNA sample. Her gaze bounced from Aidan's face to the champagne glass perched near the edge of the table. A catering attendant hovered nearby, snatching up empty glasses as if they tarnished his reputation. Emma's heartbeat echoed in her ears—and it had nothing to do with the attractive man in front of her. She had to get to that glass.

"It's good to see you. Maybe we can chat later." Emma took another step closer to the table but Aidan wrapped his fingers around her elbow and held her there.

His deep blue eyes glinted as he grinned. "Emma, I found you after all these years. Won't you at least give me one dance?"

She smiled, not wanting to hurt his feelings, and hesitated a second before responding. In that moment, the efficient catering attendant plucked Vanessa's glass from the table and scampered off to the kitchen. As Emma watched her opportunity disappear through the swinging doors, frustration bubbled beneath her calm exterior. Emma needed fresh air.

"Will you excuse me? I'll find you later. I must make a quick phone call." Emma didn't wait for a reply before heading for the exit.

She kept her head down and darted through the crowd, hoping Aidan didn't follow her to the front entrance. Outside she gulped the fresh air in deep breaths and pulled her aunt's fox wrap tightly around her shoulders as frustration surged through her. "Ma'am, are you OK?" The attendant who had opened the Caddy door for her earlier looked at her with concern. "Do you need me to get your car or find somebody for you?"

Emma smiled and shook her head. "No, I'm OK. But thank you. I needed a bit of fresh air and a minute of quiet."

"I'll leave you to it, then. I'm just a shout away if you need anything." He turned back to the valet station.

Leaning against one of the four large columns holding up the portico, Emma closed her eyes. She had been so close to getting Vanessa's DNA. If only she hadn't been distracted for that split second, she would have had the glass safely in hand.

She opened her eyes and looked at the moon shining through the trees along the border of the country club grounds.

The full moon had passed, but tonight it was still large and round enough to cast long, dark shadows of the trees on the snow. Her heartbeat returned to normal. So did her senses. What was wrong with her? She had rudely bolted away from Aidan when he'd seemed so glad to see her.

Emma's cellphone chimed inside the beaded purse dangling from her arm. She fished it out and smiled to see Kelly's number on the screen. "Hi. Aren't you supposed to be at dinner with Patrick's boss?"

"Yes, we're at a new, trendy place in Salem where the food is fabulous and the boss's wife is an utter bore. If I hear one more story of where they've been and what they've done, I'll scream," Kelly said. "I excused myself from the table to call you and prevent myself from offending her. I'm dying to know how your night is going."

Emma glanced back at the door to make sure no one was within earshot. "It's certainly not what I expected. Almost as soon as I walked in the door, I came across none other than Vanessa Nelson waving her champagne glass and quarreling with a rather agitated man. It was really something. She emptied her champagne on him and made a rather hasty exit."

"Oh, please tell me you grabbed the glass."

"Almost."

"Almost?"

Emma recounted the rest of the incident and sighed. "Aidan seemed pleased to see me, but I'm afraid I was pretty distracted. I didn't even recognize him at first."

"I guess not," Kelly said, chuckling. "It's been years since his family moved to New York City. I've not seen him in a while myself. Did you dance with him?"

"Not yet. I needed some fresh air to regain my senses after I missed the opportunity to get the glass."

"At least your evening is more exciting than mine," Kelly said. "I suppose I should get back to the table. Dessert is probably waiting for me. Go back to the ball and try to have fun."

Emma managed a smile. "Maybe dessert will make the conversation more scintillating. I'm going to look for Aidan. Thanks for calling. Good night."

She felt calmer after talking to Kelly.

She owed Aidan an apology, if not a dance. Stepping away from the column, Emma glanced at the valet station and nodded to the attendant before turning toward the door.

Emma returned to the ballroom to find the party in full swing with a packed dance floor, a line at the buffet, and people milling around in small groups. Dottie Faye was holding court by the drink station. In the small anteroom, a crowd surrounded the silent-auction table. There was no sign of Aidan. How on earth would she find him? She opted to check out the buffet table first with plans to work the perimeter of the room from there. Although she stopped from time to time to greet customers from the shop, other business owners, or friends of Dottie Faye, her eyes constantly darted in search of the red-haired Aidan.

She was close to the buffet table when she felt a hand on her back. Wheeling around, she was surprised to find a blushing Eric Hart quickly retrieving his hand.

He bent down and put his lips close to her ear. "Emma, it's good to see you. How's the ankle? You seem to be moving well, in heels no less."

"I'm good. The ankle is dealing with the heels better than my feet are at the moment. But thanks for asking."

"Are you up to a turn on the dance floor?"

Emma felt her face turning pink. "I'm really not much of a dancer. I tend to lead," she said.

"I'm happy to leave the leading to you." Just as Eric took her hand, the music slowed to a sultry ballad.

Eric led Emma to a small opening on the dance floor and took her lightly in his arms. He held her far enough away to enable them to chat comfortably. "I ran into Dottie Faye at the Wharf Seafood Restaurant earlier this week," he said. "We were both picking up carryout, and we had a nice discussion about magazines. She's quite fond of the gossip rags." Eric smiled, nodding toward the middle of the dance floor where Dottie Faye was dancing with a man at least twenty years her junior.

"That's our Dottie Faye," Emma said, watching her aunt's creative dance moves before returning her gaze to Eric. "I hope I have her spunk when I'm her age, although I am not sure exactly what that is. She's been saying she was thirty for as long as I can remember."

"She's a sport model, that's for sure. She mentioned you'd be here tonight. You know, I've had my ticket for a while. I always purchase one to support the hospital, but this is the first time I've attended in over five years."

Emma knew Eric's wife had died about five years before. While he was, according to Dottie Faye, Mystic Harbor's most eligible bachelor, evidently he'd not begun dating again. Attending the dance must have been a big step for him. "Well, I'm glad you did. I have another chance to thank you for taking care of my ankle at the festival." The music stopped and a hand appeared on Eric's shoulder. "Eric, I'm sorry to interrupt, but may I have a word with you about the new hospital wing?"

A tinge of disappointment washed over Emma as Eric let go of her hand and introduced her to Richard Strong, the president of the hospital's board of governors. "It's nice to meet you," she said, shaking his hand before turning to Eric. "Thanks for the dance."

As the band led into a fast pop song, Emma made her way to the cascading drink fountain. She was ready to sip punch, sit down, and people-watch for a while. What a night. First she had blown a great chance to get a DNA sample from Vanessa, and then she had slighted a man she'd not seen since childhood. To top it off, she'd prattled on to Eric about her feet. Eric might be tied up for the evening, but maybe she'd see Aidan again so she could apologize for her rude behavior.

Drink in hand, Emma sank into a chair at an empty table along the edge of the dance floor and marveled as Dottie Faye danced with another much younger man. Her aunt was the stuff legends were made of. She stared in awe as another handsome, tuxedo-clad young man cut in for his turn to dance with the daring Dottie Faye. But her admiration turned to irritation when she saw Dottie Faye point a rhinestone-laden finger directly at her and wave. The man grinned and turned back to her aunt with a nod.

Understanding washed over Emma as her aunt's last partner headed toward the table. Everything was a set up—the tickets, the outfit, Dottie Faye's insistence that she attend the ball. It was all designed to get her here to be displayed like an overage debutante. And Maeve had given Aidan a ticket, so she was part of this charade too. How could they do this?

Propelled by anger and embarrassment, Emma crossed the dance floor.

"May I cut in?" she said, tapping Dottie Faye's dance partner on the shoulder.

"Sure," he said, his eyes roaming the length of Emma's gown.

"No, I mean I want to talk to my aunt. In private. Please excuse us." Emma grasped Dottie Faye by the forearm and pulled her off the dance floor. "We're going to the powder room. Now."

Emma wordlessly propelled Dottie Faye to the powder room. Once inside, she let go of her aunt's arm. "How many?"

"Emma Jane, whatever do you mean, 'how many?'" Dottie Faye batted her heavily mascaraed lashes and pressed the fingers of her right hand against her chest.

"Don't play innocent with me. You know exactly what I mean. How many men did you arrange to dance with me besides Eric Hart and Kelly's cousin Aidan?" Emma struggled to keep her voice low. "How could you embarrass me like this?"

Dottie Faye's eyes softened, and she wrapped her black feather boa tighter around her arms. "I wasn't trying to embarrass you. After all, you're my own flesh and blood. I was simply helping you move on with your life." She blinked her eyes, and it looked like crocodile tears were forming beneath the lids. "You've not dated since you and Josh called off your wedding. It's been years. I just want you to be happy, sugar plum."

"I know you mean well, Dottie Faye. I really do. But I don't need a man to make me happy." Emma opened the door of the powder room. "Are we clear on that?"

Emma shifted her purse to her left hand and kept her wrap closed with the other as she bolted to the front exit, Dottie Faye at her heels.

"Emma, wait." Eric strode through the foyer as the two women turned and paused in the doorway. "Could we … umm … maybe meet for coffee next week?"

His words hung in the air as Emma contemplated what to say.

Dottie Faye firmly planted her elbow in Emma's side. "Answer him, Emma Jane."

"Sure. OK," Emma stammered, feeling like a hunted animal caught in the headlights of a four-wheel drive. "Call me."

six

Two streetlamps flickered in the darkening sky, throwing eerie shadows from two giant elm trees flanking the old brownstone apartment building where Vanessa Nelson lived. Emma and Kelly lingered in front of the building, trying to look inconspicuous.

"I tried to get her apartment number yesterday, but none of the volunteers had ever been here." Kelly looked up, as if looking up would determine which window belonged to Vanessa's unit.

"Don't do that. You look like a peeping Tom or something. Try to act natural," Emma chided. "Someone is bound to come along soon. We can follow them into the lobby. When the coast is clear, we can find her name and apartment number on the mailbox."

"And you think holding large boxes and loitering outside an apartment building makes us look natural?" Kelly snickered.

Emma moved her fingers along the bottom of the box to keep them from getting cramped. "Maybe not, but the boxes give a person a good reason to hold the door open for us so we can get inside the security door."

"Have you thought about how we will busy ourselves and not look suspicious until this person leaves the lobby?" Kelly drummed her fingers on the box top. "Don't you think we will look a bit silly wandering aimlessly while he checks his mail or searches for his key?"

Emma cleared her throat and gestured at a man who had just passed them and was clearing the first of two sets of steps on the walkway to Vanessa's building. Scampering behind him, Emma and Kelly reached the door in time to ask him to hold it for them.

"Thank you," said Emma, breezing through the door in front of him.

Rubbing his hands from the cold, he walked straight to the stairwell door and held it ajar too.

"Oh, you go ahead, my phone is vibrating," Kelly said, setting the box down and removing her cellphone from her purse. "I'd better take this before we go up. Thanks anyway."

When the door closed behind him, Emma scanned the bank of mailboxes lining the wall on the opposite end of the lobby. "Here it is. Nelson, number 306. Thank goodness there's an elevator. There will be less chance of meeting up with someone who might question why we're here."

They left the boxes on a rectangular table near the mailboxes and walked to the elevator.

"Are you surprised about the elevator? Vanessa doesn't strike me as the type who would take the stairs. The exertion might wilt her power suits." Kelly pressed the elevator button and the doors opened right away.

"She's not that bad, especially for someone who might be a thief or murderer," Emma said as she stepped into the elevator.

They rode the squeaky elevator in silence. Emma hoped the thing didn't stall, especially when they were so close to finding some answers from Vanessa. She didn't have any desire to spend the night cooped up in an antique elevator, even with her best friend.

Emma breathed a sigh of relief when the elevator doors opened. She was also pleased to find Vanessa's apartment two doors down the hall. Coming to a halt before apartment 306, she glanced at Kelly and rapped on the door three times.

She heard the sound of a chain sliding into place before the door opened about an inch. Emma wondered if Vanessa had looked out the peephole.

"Yes?" Vanessa's voice sounded tentative.

"Vanessa, it's Emma and Kelly, the museum volunteers. Remember us?"

"I do. Why are you here? Are you cops or something? News reporters?"

"We were friends of Rose Peterson, and we'd like to talk to you about her," Kelly replied. "That's why we were at the museum."

Vanessa closed the door to unchain the lock before opening it wide enough for Emma and Kelly to enter the apartment. "You knew Rose? No wonder you were so stunned when you saw my rose quilt in the office. I knew you appreciated good quilt designs when you saw them, but I've not had anyone react that way to my work."

She ushered them through a small foyer and into a large living room. While the wood floors, beige walls and white trim were neutral, an eclectic mix of artwork added splashes of color to the room. Emma and Kelly sank down in a cushy, camel-colored sofa in front of a coffee table holding a fan of various art magazines and an abstract bronze sculpture. The orderly living space appealed to Emma's perfectionist side.

Although Vanessa didn't offer to take their coats, Emma shrugged out of hers and draped it over the arm of the sofa before taking a seat. Kelly laid hers on top of it and sat next to Emma.

Vanessa perched, unmoving, in the chair across from them while Emma and Kelly took turns relating their stories about Rose, recounting a few of their childhood adventures, their mutual love of art and quilts, and the grief brought by her death.

"Each year around the anniversary of her death, I make a pilgrimage to the local police department in hopes of finding out something new, but the detective on the case never seems to have anything," Emma said. She put her tote bag on her lap and lifted out a square of muslin. "Last year I came across an old quilt Rose's mom had given me after the funeral. I'd put it in a closet without opening the bag. It was too painful."

Emma handed the square to Vanessa. "I think you'll remember this. You had an eye for design even back then."

Vanessa laid the fabric across her lap and smoothed it against her denim-clad thigh. She rubbed her hand along the angular rose petals pieced together to give a stained glass effect and made a short, quiet, laughing sound. "Oh, but my stitches were so uneven, and the petals are puckered. Yet Rose was so encouraging … she always was. To everyone."

Kelly cleared her throat and leaned forward. "Vanessa, we believe Rose was killed by someone in that quilting class. We know for sure she was afraid of someone at the time."

"Surely you don't believe I had something to do with her death. She was my mentor, my friend. She encouraged my love of fiber arts and gave me a career path." Eyes blazing, Vanessa jumped up, sending the quilt square tumbling to the floor. "This is simply outrageous."

Emma raised her eyebrows. Vanessa sure was overreacting to Kelly's comment. "We're not accusing you of anything. We've cleared four of your former classmates through DNA samples. We'd like to clear you too, and talk about what you remember from that last day of Rose's class." She pulled a DNA collection kit from her tote. "It only takes seconds to get a swab of the inside of your cheek, and it's painless, I promise."

Silence filled the room until Kelly began drumming her fingertips on the glass-top end table next to her. The collection kit, weighing just a few ounces, seemed heavy in Emma's hand.

Finally Vanessa spoke. "I'll give you a sample and tell you what I saw on the night Rose was killed."

Tested to the limit of her patience, Emma let out a short breath and lifted the kit to open the plastic bag. "Thank you. We really—"

"Let me finish." Vanessa stopped pacing and looked down at Emma. "I'll do this for you, but in return, you have to help me clear my name at the museum. Do that, and then I'll tell you what I know and submit to your test. I didn't commit murder—or steal anything."

Emma and Kelly stared at each other with wide eyes and open mouths. The plastic bag still dangled from Emma's hand. Vanessa didn't seem to notice.

"I don't have any idea who stole the painting or why Kayla and Gabe think it was me. But I have a good idea who killed Rose," Vanessa said, cutting eyes first to Emma and then to Kelly. "It'll not only surprise *you*, it will set the whole world on fire. It's huge, I tell you."

Emma lowered the DNA sample kit but didn't return it to her tote. "This is bribery, you know."

"Emma, let's be rational about this," Kelly said. "I recognize that look on your face. Be reasonable. Vanessa has information we need. We can get information she needs. It's as simple as that."

Vanessa scoffed. "I prefer to think of it as a mutually beneficial arrangement. A tribute to Rose, if you will." Vanessa bent down, picked up the quilt square, and tossed it on the coffee table. "Clearly, you have things to decide. I'll let you two discuss my offer in private while I call in a dinner reservation. For one."

Vanessa disappeared down a hallway. Emma and Kelly didn't speak until they heard a door close at the other end.

"I think we should help her," Kelly said. "How else are we going to get a DNA sample? We've already tried twice."

Emma shook her head. "No, because we can't be sure she will give us the sample or the information once she's cleared—if she's ever cleared. We need to make sure she's not the murderer before we spend time solving the theft. Solving Rose's murder is our main goal here."

"So what do you suggest?"

Emma took a deep breath as she heard the door open and shut again. She leaned closer to Kelly. "A counteroffer."

Emma felt the room grow chilly as Vanessa swept into it.

"So, when will you start your investigation into the theft?" Vanessa stood with hands on her hips.

"As soon as you give us a DNA sample and it proves you didn't kill Rose." Emma's voice was calm and even. "Then we will do what we can to help clear you of the theft charges."

"You are a tough one, Emma," Vanessa said. "But it's a deal."

Emma smiled and handed the DNA kit to Kelly. "Would you like to do the honors?"

Two minutes later, the sample taken and safely tucked into Kelly's bag, the women began discussing the museum theft, with Emma and Kelly firing off questions and Vanessa answering some of them. Vanessa reiterated she had no idea why Gabe Lucier and Kayla Turner believed she had stolen the painting. Nor could she think of anyone at the museum who had any reason to see her framed for theft and thus taken out of the picture. "After all, I am good at my job," said Vanessa, as if that alone proved her innocence.

"You're not giving us much to go on," Emma finally said.

"Do you have any idea why the police department wasn't involved in investigating the theft?"

"That I can answer," Vanessa said. She stood up and began pacing behind her chair. "But you have to promise me it won't go any further. I know I will eventually be cleared of this theft because I didn't do it; but if word got out that I told you about private museum business, my career would be over."

"Vanessa, you're going to have to trust someone. Since we're trying to help you, it may as well be us." Kelly's stomach was audibly growling, and Emma could tell she was getting impatient. "The more information we have, the faster we can solve this mystery."

Vanessa sighed and returned to the chair. "OK, OK. Gabe and Kayla have been working for years to bring a very prestigious and valuable exhibit to the museum. They are close to finalizing the deal and putting it on the calendar." For the first time, Vanessa gave some hint of vulnerability. "Police involvement would attract the press."

"And negative press would kill any chances of finalizing the deal," Emma concluded. "One more question. Who were you arguing with at the hospital ball Saturday night? I tried to talk to you, but you threw a drink in his face and ran out before I could catch you."

"That would have been my ex-boyfriend, Matthew Goodman. He chose the biggest social event of the year to pick a fight. We broke up six months ago. I'd not seen him since then until he accosted me at the ball."

"Is he mad enough to frame you for theft?" Emma glanced at her watch. They were running out of time to get the DNA sample to the lab before it closed.

"Hardly. He wanted his electric razor back. He accused me of stealing it." An amused smile tugged at the corners of her mouth. "I didn't steal it. I merely threw it in the dumpster."

Emma searched Vanessa's face for signs of emotion. She didn't see any and wasn't quite sure what to say. This seemed like as good a time as any to end the conversation. "I guess we've taken up enough of your time for one day." She grabbed the coats as she walked to the door. "We'll be in touch soon."

By the time Emma had unlocked the front door of her cottage that night, the temperature had dropped twenty degrees, and the wind had hurled a layer of debris onto her small porch. She was tired and irritated with Vanessa for not sharing the details she knew about the night Rose had died, but at least the DNA sample was safely at the lab for testing. Most likely, they'd know the results by the next evening. Thank goodness reason had overridden fatigue, motivating Emma and Kelly to rush by the lab after leaving Vanessa. They'd barely made it.

She sighed while stepping over the threshold. It was good to be home after such a long, trying day. After hanging her jacket on the coat rack and dropping her bags on its lower shelf, she headed toward the kitchen to fix a cup of tea. Her relief turned to a chill when she realized her family photos had been rearranged on the long rectangular table in the foyer and the light by her fireside reading chair had been turned on. Her skin crawled.

Someone had been in the cottage. Were they still there? Closing her eyes, Emma forced her mind and breathing to slow so she could concentrate on the sounds in the dim rooms.

Silence, until the refrigerator motor kicked on. After several seconds, she crept closer to the fireplace, her heart pounding harder with each step.

Her breath caught in her throat when she saw the deep red package under the reading lamp. Should she call the police? No, not until she could tell them what it was. When she was a little farther than an arm's length away, Emma realized a card was leaning against the front of the box. She leaned forward and grasped the card, letting it fall to the ground as soon as she saw the drops of blood drawn on the outside. Her brain told her to call 911. Her curiosity ordered her to unwrap the package. Without lifting the box from the table, Emma slid her fingernails under the tape at either end, and then peeled back the paper. She tossed the wrapping onto the chair. Emma placed both hands around the lid and cautiously lifted it off the box.

Nestled inside was a red velvet box, which Emma—encouraged since the package hadn't blown up—plucked from its tissue paper nest. She inhaled and held her breath as she opened the box to find a pair of deep red glass teardrop earrings and a matching bracelet.

Emma collapsed into the chair and landed on the wrapping paper, still holding the box. She'd received some strange items in boxes since beginning her investigation into Rose's death, but this was the first one containing mystery jewelry. She looked at the design—creepy blood drops made of high-quality fused glass and sterling silver. Where had they come from?

She reached down to the floor and retrieved the envelope and stared at the inked blood drips. After a few moments, she tore the top off the envelope and removed the card. Ten seconds later, she began laughing as she read, "I'm feeling blue because I made you turn red. I love you. Dottie Faye"

They weren't blood drops—they were tears.

Emma retrieved the cellphone from her purse and punched the speed-dial number for her aunt. Her fear and irritation vanished when she heard the Southern drawl on the other end of the phone.

"I love you too, Dottie Faye, even if you almost scared me to death."

seven

As soon as the first light of dawn provided enough visibility to safely run along neighborhood streets the next morning, Emma layered her cold-weather running gear, laced up her new shoes, and skipped down the walkway to the road. She loved running at dawn, when she shared the road with only the paper deliverers, garbage men, and an occasional early riser strolling to the end of the driveway to retrieve the daily newspaper. Quiet solitude was necessary to collect her thoughts and prepare for the day. *Why is it*, she wondered, *that people have such a difficult time understanding such a simple concept?*

She knew Dottie Faye meant well and only wanted her to be happy. Happiness, to Dottie Faye, meant getting plenty of attention from men. But women really didn't need a man to be successful and happy these days. Right?

Emma waved to the couple delivering papers as the wife slowed the car and the husband prepared to toss a bagged copy onto a nearby driveway. She watched the car pull ahead of her and the brake lights flash at the next house. What would it be like to have someone around to help with household chores, accompany her to concerts, or fix her soup when she had the flu? *Would that cramp my style?* The thought kicked her into a sprint that lasted well over a block. When she slowed back down to a jog, Eric Hart flashed across her mind. She had to admit, she'd been a bit disappointed when their dance was interrupted. But did she even have time in her life for dating? Not now. But maybe after Rose's murder was solved.

Her head cleared by running, Emma thought of the day's possibilities. Kelly would be late getting to the shop; she was stopping by the museum to talk with her friends in the gift shop. Hopefully that would generate leads on the theft. And if they were lucky, the results of Vanessa's DNA test would be in hand before the end of the day. Emma wasn't convinced the ice queen was innocent, even though she did seem genuinely thankful for all that Rose had taught her.

As Emma turned back onto her street for the last leg of her run, two screaming hawks circled above her. A shudder swept over her as she slowed to a fast walk and looked up. There was something hauntingly beautiful about these birds of prey.

The shudder turned quickly to fear and then to anger at what she saw when she turned up the walkway to her cottage.

"Hey!" she shouted to the black-clad prowler crouching on her porch, peering into the window. "What do you think you're doing?"

He leaped down the steps, colliding with Emma and knocking her to the ground. She managed to grab his black knitted hood as she fell, but she didn't get a look at his face. Shaking off the pain, she jumped to her feet and tore off after him. But by the end of the block, Emma had lost her assailant.

Emma collected her wits. Her cheek stung where she'd skinned it on the sidewalk. She thought of all the times she'd been chased, hit, held at gunpoint, and burglarized since beginning the quest to find Rose's killer. *When is this going to stop?*

The shop bell jangled and Emma looked up from the counter to see Tokala Abrams enter with her thin arms wrapped around a fat bag.

Tokala hurried in, her eyes sparkling like new copper pennies. They darkened when she was close enough to see Emma's face.

"Ouch, what happened to you?" Tokala, a pharmacist accustomed to giving advice about medications, instinctively reached over the counter toward the side of Emma's face. "Have you been fighting with the pavement again? You need to put something on that scrape."

Emma responded by taking a quick step back. "After my run this morning, the sidewalk slapped me when a prowler knocked me down outside my home. I washed out the scrape and dabbed some antiseptic on it. I'm OK." She gestured at Tokala's arms. "What do you have there? That looks suspiciously like a bag from Uncommon Threads."

Tokala grinned. "It is. My niece Nikki is graduating from high school in May. I've been trying to find the perfect gift for her." She placed the bag on the counter and pulled out several pieces of fabric and lined them up across the counter. "Nikki is very interested in the Native American side of our family and recently discovered her animal totems. Look at these fabrics. Aren't the rich colors beautiful?"

A forest of animals stretched across the wood counter, from lizards and turtles to wolves and bears. There was one lone bird, an owl. One solid fabric, a dark blue with gray threads running through, coordinated with all the patterns. Emma assumed this would be the quilt backing.

Emma held up each fabric individually and studied the weight, color, and design. "What a touching graduation gift for Nikki. She will pass it down to her kids one day."

"Yes, I hope so." Tokala gazed at the fabric for a moment. "Indian folklore says we are all connected to nine animal totems that come in and out of our lives, depending on where we are in our journey of life. Nikki and I share two, the turtle and the wolf, but I'm going to include all nine in her quilt."

"Those seem like two totally different types of animals," said Emma, her brows furrowed.

"According to legend, each animal provides something different and appears when its trait is needed. The turtle represents nurturing and protection. The wolf symbolizes loyalty and intuition."

Returning the fabric to the paper bag, Tokala sighed. "These aren't the only gorgeous fabrics Marcia has among her new arrivals. You should see the new line of fruit-inspired Roman Originals. The man is a genius."

Emma had read rave reviews about Antonio Roman's Dew Kist fruit-inspired line but hadn't had a chance to see it firsthand. "I'll have to stop by to see Marcia and check it out. I've been too preoccupied lately."

"How's the investigation going? Anything new besides that bad scrape?" Tokala's eyes drifted to Emma's scrape.

The door bells chimed again, announcing Kelly's arrival.

"Ah, just in the nick of time," Emma said as the door closed. "Tokala was asking for an update on the investigation. Did the girls in the gift shop give you any good leads?"

Kelly frowned as she approached the counter. "What happened to your face?"

Emma told Kelly about the prowler incident. Kelly in turn explained to Tokala what they'd learned from Vanessa the previous night.

"Do you think Emma's prowler this morning has anything

to do with your visit with Vanessa Nelson last night?" Tokala's eyes drifted from Kelly to Emma. "Sometimes answers don't come in words but in actions."

Kelly leaned closer to Emma. "Tokala is right, Emma. We don't really know what kind of person we are dealing with in Vanessa. Maybe you should restrict your running to daylight hours for now.

Emma didn't want to debate her running habits. "Let's sit down," she said, motioning to the comfy chairs in the alcove. "So, what did you find out at the museum?"

Kelly held up a black bag with a white kettle logo. "As long as you don't mind if we snack at the same time. I brought chocolate croissants from The Chocolate Cauldron."

Tokala and Emma declined a treat and waited while Kelly took a bite of her croissant.

"Well?" Emma asked impatiently.

"I didn't find out much. The museum director must have issued a gag order on discussing the situation because everyone was pretty buttoned up about it."

Emma closed her eyes and rubbed her temples with her forefingers. "I was afraid of that."

"I suppose I can't blame the museum administration for not allowing gossip about such a serious subject," said Tokala. "After all, they have a reputation to maintain."

"But I have more," Kelly said.

"Oh, please do tell." Emma was unsuccessful in keeping impatience out of her voice.

Kelly leaned forward, her face registering the same excitement as Dottie Faye's did when she was repeating stories about Hollywood scandals. "Cammie Smythe and I went to the ladies' room to wash up after I helped her haul boxes from the storeroom to the display cases. When we were away from her boss and the other volunteers, I asked her if anyone had a reason to frame Vanessa for the theft."

"And?" Emma asked.

"Maybe she was framed. The rumor mill believes the curator's assistant, Claire Blevins, would be ecstatic if Vanessa was fired. Cammie and her mother, Catherine Hamilton, believe that Claire Blevins, the assistant to the curator, has battled some pretty intense jealousy issues. Evidently, she's had her eye on Vanessa's job since completing her master's degree several months ago. Evidently she is ready to move up the organizational chart."

Emma's eyes widened. "Well, that's at least something to consider."

"Yes, except Claire was out on a six-week medical leave when the painting disappeared. She wasn't even around."

"Appearances can be deceptive," said Tokala. "Maybe you need to find out more about Claire's illness and her feelings about Vanessa."

Kelly rolled the top of the croissant bag closed and stood up. "I suppose you're right. We'll have a chance to snoop around on Monday during our next volunteer shift."

After bending down to retrieve her bag of fabric, Tokala stood to leave. "I know you're troubled and anxious to find the truth about what happened to your friend. An old Native American saying tells us to speak the truth quietly, to listen with an open mind when others speak, and to remember the truth and peace that may be found in silence." She walked to the door, stopped, and turned around. "Truth is often obscured by illusion. Someone out there knows what happened to Rose."

When the door closed behind Tokala, Kelly placed her hand on Emma's shoulder. "We will find out the truth, you know. We have to keep rattling cages."

"I know," Emma said. "Speaking of rattling cages, your mom called today and asked when we were going to start decorating for St. Patrick's Day. Think we're prepared to handle the Dottie Faye explosion when she sees we've replaced her hearts with Maeve's shamrocks?"

Kelly picked up a pink heart-shaped dish Dottie Faye had placed on the checkout counter. "Do you think it would appease her if we point out the fact that each shamrock contains three hearts?"

"Appease Dottie Faye with anything that relates to your mom? Surely you jest."

"Oh, I don't know." Kelly snickered. "They worked dangerously well together in plotting to jump-start your love life at the country club."

Emma wadded up one of Dottie Faye's paper doily hearts and hurled it at Kelly. "I don't want to discuss my so-called love life. It was scary how easily they pulled that off right under my nose. Next time, give me a heads-up, OK?"

"Something tells me we don't have to worry about the two of them being in cahoots for St. Patrick's Day," Kelly said, tossing Emma's doily ball into the air and catching it.

"I hope you're right. I think I like them better as adversaries than co-conspirators."

Drumming her fingers on the counter, Kelly opened her mouth to say something but closed it without saying a word. Emma knew that wasn't a good sign. "OK, spill it. What are you trying not to say?"

"Oh, I will be dead meat if I tell you," Kelly groaned. "Mom has a surprise for you this year."

"Does it involve Dottie Faye?"

"No. It's something Mom has been working on for weeks. By herself. No Dottie Faye. You'll love it, so put your mind at ease. But I'm serious; she won't be amused if I tell you. You'll be happy to know it doesn't involve any men except St. Patrick."

"That's a relief," said Emma. "I'll be even more relieved when we get the results from Vanessa's DNA test. Patience has never been my strong point."

"No kidding." Kelly replied. "I'm a bit surprised you've not called the lab yet."

"Give me time," Emma chuckled.

They spent the rest of the afternoon packing up some of Dottie Faye's Valentine's Day decorations, working up an estimate for restoring an old family quilt for a woman Emma had spoken to earlier in the morning, and searching through catalogs for new spring lines. Emma had started her to-do list for the next day and Kelly had begun closing up the shop when their trusty old fax machine squealed and spit out several sheets.

Kelly scampered to the machine and leafed through the pages. "Emma, I guess we're one step closer to the truth."

eight

Emma melted into one of Marcia's overstuffed chairs in the quilting room and let the act of creating perfectly sized and spaced stitches work their magic. At long last she was returning to work on the T-shirt quilt made of squares from her collection of participant T-shirts gathered over years of running in races. She'd come up with the idea months ago, before plunging headlong onto the trail of a murderer.

Making the running quilt enabled her to clean out her closet without throwing away mementoes of well-run races. It was a perfect way to remove clutter, and Emma hated clutter with a passion. As she concentrated on a purple-and-black square commemorating a personal best in the last Mystic Harbor Magical Mystery Run, the hum of conversation among the quilters soothed her soul. It had been a long week and she was grateful for a chance to relax with friends.

"Wow, I see you dug your running quilt squares out from the mothballs," Kelly said, leaning over for a closer look. "I haven't seen you work on it in ages."

Emma pulled another stitch through the fabric and smiled. "I've been a bit preoccupied, that's for sure."

"I guess both of us have had Rose on our minds a lot lately." Kelly pulled a bundle of fabric quarters and a pair of scissors out of her tote bag and stood up. "But each day we get closer to the truth," she said, taking a step toward the nearby worktable occupied by Maeve, who was finishing up details on a secret quilt project.

The hum of the sewing machine stopped and Marcia turned around in her chair to face Emma. "Do you have any news on that front?"

Emma and Kelly told about their visit with Vanessa, recounting their frustration with her initial refusal to give them a DNA sample, and her holding hostage the information about the night of Rose's death until they cleared her of the museum theft charge.

"Isn't that a type of extortion?" Marcia frowned. "Did you agree to it?"

"Emma was brilliant," Kelly said with a snicker. "She forced Vanessa's hand by refusing to help her unless she allowed us to swab her cheek."

"And?" Walter shifted the tulips and daisies on his lap. "Do tell. What were the results?"

Kelly glanced at Emma and raised her eyebrows. Emma bobbed her chin. "You do the honors, Kelly."

"Her DNA results didn't match the sample taken from under Rose's fingernails. That removes her from our suspect list." Kelly sighed. "She claims to have some sort of important details about the night Rose died, but she is refusing to give us any more information until we find out who stole the painting from the museum. Vanessa still maintains it was a setup."

The sound of high heels clacking on the steps sounded up the stairway. "Yoo-hoo, everyone. I'm here." Dottie Faye pranced into the room while shrugging out of her white fur jacket. "I was waylaid by the absolutely scrumptious specimen of a man walking a hideously large dog on Main Street."

She looked pointedly at Emma, who pretended not to notice. Emma was getting weary of her aunt's insinuations about available men and her need to latch onto one. She was fine on her own. Glancing around the room, Emma hoped someone would distract Dottie Faye's attention from playing matchmaker. She caught Walter's eye, and he winked.

"Dottie Faye, how nice to see you. Your timing is impeccable as always," said Walter, his quiet demeanor contrasting with the Southern belle's flamboyance. "Emma and Kelly are about to give us an update on the murder investigation."

Waving her hand toward Emma, Dottie Faye tossed her teased head. "I know about the DNA results. I *am* Emma's aunt, after all. What I want to know is what you are going to do next. Who do you think stole the painting?" Dottie Faye pulled a folding chair from the worktable and pushed it closer to Emma.

"We're not exactly sure." Emma continued stitching the Magical Mystery square with a steady cadence. "But the front-runner seems to be the curator's assistant, Claire Blevins. Rumor has it she has been gunning for Vanessa's job. But it seems she's been on medical leave for several weeks, so we have some digging to do."

"Oh, how positively boring." Dottie Faye pulled a copy of *Hollywood Dish* magazine from her nearly empty craft bag. "I think she is being set up by a disgruntled lover. Just like Desiree Bennet and Max Powers and the spat they had while filming the world's best soap, *The Days of Forever*. She tried to get him fired—and here they were supposed to love each other." Dottie Faye flipped to a centerfold photo of Desiree and her new man and gazed at it as if this was proof of Vanessa's guilt. "Didn't you see that scene Vanessa made at the ball, flinging a drink in that poor man's face and all? I tell you, this is a crime of passion, pure and simple."

"Dottie Faye, that is absolutely absurd. We are talking about the arts community of Boston here, not some sleazy soap opera set filled with raging hormones," said Maeve, lifting her eyes from her secret project for the first time. She was sitting at the table on the far side of Tokala. "But I admit I'm bothered by Vanessa's coercing our Kelly and Emma into clearing her name. It seems underhanded to me."

Marcia turned from her silent sewing machine. "Maybe this has all been a misunderstanding. What if the painting has just been misplaced by a volunteer or even by Claire before she left on medical leave?"

The bright sun that had filtered through the large windows disappeared behind clouds, and the room became darker despite the early hour. Marcia got up from the sewing table and switched on several lamps before returning to her seat. Emma wished someone could turn on a light and illuminate all of the answers they needed to solve Rose's murder. Why did each clue seem to lead to another question shrouded in shadows?

"I thought of that too, Marcia, but how does someone lose a painting? After talking to Vanessa a few times, I've also wondered if someone from Vanessa's past had the painting stolen to settle some sort of vendetta. Vanessa is so icy, it makes me question what happened in her past to make her that way. Maybe that something motivated someone to take action against her," Emma said.

Walter held up his nearly finished quilt top, and the flower-laden squares tumbled toward the floor. He folded it over several times and put it in the satchel at his feet before leaning back in his chair and scratching his head. "It seems to me the first thing you need to do is befriend Claire, find out more about her absence, and determine her relationship with Vanessa before you eliminate either one of them as a suspect," he said. "It could be that they're in this together."

The quilters fell quiet, each one seeming to let Walter's suggestion sink in before voicing another suggestion. After a minute or so, Tokala broke the silence in her calm, logical way.

"I suggest you keep a chart of suspects and note the motive and opportunity for each one," she said, lifting the image of a wolf from the piece of fabric she was cutting. "Having a visual of the relationships will help you separate truth from illusion."

Keeping her head bowed to her work, Emma's brain went into overdrive as she tried to sort the few clues they had and match them to the suspects. She needed to think without so many people around her. "Kelly, I just remembered we need to be at the shop for a delivery this morning. Want to come?" Emma stared at Kelly and cut her eyes to the door. Luckily, it seemed that everyone else had returned to focusing on quilting.

Kelly winked. "Sure. You don't need to be handling all of that yourself." She returned to the chair near Emma and stuffed her fabric into her tote.

After collecting their belongings and saying their goodbyes, Emma and Kelly headed downstairs into the showroom, where they stopped for a minute to admire the display of Roman Originals fabric before leaving the shop.

"We're getting awfully good at this nonverbal communication," said Kelly while stepping off the curb onto Main Street.

"We should be," Emma replied. "We've been perfecting 'The Stare' for decades."

"Very true. But why the hasty exit?"

"I wanted to plan our next move without an audience," Emma said. "I'm thinking about what Tokala said about creating a chart. We have one for Rose; why not make one for the museum theft too? It will keep us organized."

Emma and Kelly exchanged greetings with several shopkeepers and customers as they crossed the square, which was now bare of both snow and greenery. Emma cringed when they passed the spot where she had taken her "bow" to Cupid, but she kept her thoughts to herself because so many people were on the path. They were about to cross Gallows Way when they finally had some privacy.

"We need to get everything straight in our minds before we volunteer at the museum on Monday," said Emma, digging her keys out of her bag before stepping into the road. "After charting all of the persons of interest, we'll know what to do next."

"Makes sense," said Kelly, picking up the pace as a car approached. "It will keep us focused."

They stepped onto the sidewalk in front of Cotton & Grace and Emma handed the shop keys to Kelly. "If you open up, I'll treat us to coffee to fuel our charting."

"Add a muffin and it's a deal," said Kelly, plucking the keys from Emma's fingers.

Emma shook her head. "You are incorrigible. Why don't you weigh three hundred pounds?"

"Good genes, I always say. I'll have everything open when you get here."

Kelly vanished into the Cotton & Grace storefront as Emma turned toward Grounds for Suspicion. A teenage boy Emma didn't recognize smiled and held the door for her as she entered the coffeehouse and followed her inside. The usual morning crowd was bunched together in front of the pastry display case as customers jockeyed for position to see the day's selection. Emma perused the sweet treats and decided on an apple muffin for Kelly, before forcing herself to bypass a blueberry scone.

Several people left at one time and the crowd abruptly shifted forward, propelling Emma into a tall man who was squeezing by her with a cup of coffee and a doughnut in his hands. When she looked up to apologize for making him spill his coffee, she found herself staring into the hazel eyes and weathered face of Deputy Chief Tom Boyer, the detective who had investigated Rose's death and rather grudgingly tolerated Emma's annual visits to the police department.

"Good morning, Deputy Chief," she said, rooting around in her purse for a clean tissue. "I'm so sorry I made you spill your coffee. The crowd is particularly impatient today." She proffered the tissue. "Here. This is clean. I promise."

His eyes narrowed as he rested his doughnut on the top of his cup, pulled the tissue from Emma's fingers, and wiped the back of the hand grasping his coffee. "How are you these days, Miss Cotton? Staying out of trouble?"

"I'm well, thanks. Have you made any headway in solving Rose's murder?"

Drumming his fingers on the coffee cup, Boyer cast his eyes longingly toward the door. "Now, Miss Cotton, you know the department has other unsolved cases to investigate. We don't have time to reopen old accidental-death investigations. We've been over this."

Emma resisted the urge to put her hand on his arm to stop him from shifting his weight back and forth. "Have there been any problems with art theft in the area?"

The leg shifting stopped. "No, all's been quiet on the art-world front. Why do you ask?"

"Oh, you know my aunt, Dottie Faye. She hears one little piece of gossip about an ex-husband stealing a friend's painting, and the next thing you know, she's cooked up an art theft ring," Emma said, hoping the deputy chief didn't notice her hesitation before the fib slithered off her tongue.

"Art theft. Are you sleuthing full time these days?"

Emma's eyes rose to meet his. "I'm still chasing Rose's killer, if that's what you mean. But quilting is my business," she replied.

"Just remember, Miss Cotton, it isn't wise to take the law into your own hands."

The cashier called Emma's name and motioned her toward the register to pay. The muffin was sitting in a bag on the counter next to two cups of coffee.

"Just in the nick of time," said Susie, the cashier. "You looked like you needed saving. Deputy Chief Boyer can be an old coot when he wants to be."

"True," said Emma as she handed Susie a couple of bills. "Keep the change."

"Now spill it, Kelly Ann. What were you two hiding from the Nimble Thimbles?" Dottie Faye's voice filtered out of Cotton & Grace as Emma pushed open the door while carefully balancing the coffee cups and muffin bag. She should have known her aunt would show up wanting more details about Vanessa.

"Dottie Faye, if I had known you were coming by, I would have brought you a cup of coffee too," Emma said as she crossed the room and placed one cup and the bag into Kelly's outstretched hand. She tried to act surprised to see her aunt. Truth be told, Emma would have been amazed if Dottie Faye *hadn't* stopped by to pump them for more information. Dottie Faye loved a good mystery nearly as much as steamy gossip.

"I tried to tell her we weren't keeping anything from her, but Dottie Faye wouldn't listen." Kelly put her goodies on the counter before carefully pulling the top off the muffin and placing the bottom in the bag.

"I see."

Emma disappeared into the back office and reappeared with a large piece of the drawing paper she used to sketch out quilt designs. Across the top she wrote the words "Suspect," "Motive," "Opportunity," "Alibi," and "Connection to Vanessa." She printed the names "Vanessa Nelson" and "Claire Blevins" neatly under the "Suspect" heading and held the paper up for Dottie Faye to see. "This is what we came back to do. Tokala was right; this will help us stay organized and focused. We'll hang it in the office and add to it as we go."

"It looks somewhat anemic," said Kelly, leaning over the counter for a closer look. "But we should have more information to add after our volunteer shift on Monday."

Silence hung in the air for a moment until Dottie Faye grabbed the chart and waved it in front of Emma's face. "You'll have more details to add if you let me tag along on your volunteer shift. My new conversation magnifier from SuperSleuther. com arrived yesterday, and I'm dying to try it out."

"Dottie Faye, you can bat those glittered fake eyelashes all you want, but the answer is still no. Getting additional information will take finesse." Emma snatched the paper from her aunt's fingers. "And we all know subtlety is not your strong point. Besides, we need you to open the shop for us."

Kelly cleared her throat, a grin slowly spreading across her face. "Oh, I don't know, Emma. Perhaps we should hear more about this conversation magnifier before we make any rash decisions."

"Oh no you don't. Don't encourage her. And we need to get to work. We need to finish the church quilt restoration," Emma said, tossing her head in the direction of a colorful quilt draped across the worktable.

"That's OK, I need to get going. I have things to do," Dottie

Faye said as she pulled on her jacket and grabbed the matching purse. She walked to the door and opened it but turned and looked back at Emma and Kelly with a grin. "I'll see you tomorrow."

nine

"He certainly is handsome," Kelly said. She and Emma had walked up to the side entrance of the museum the following Monday to find Jake Allen deep in animated conversation with an attractive woman sporting a brown leather jacket and matching skirt with tights. "I wonder who she is? I don't remember seeing her last time we were here."

"I guess we'll find out soon enough," said Emma, ignoring the comment about Jake. She was getting weary of everyone pointing out every eligible man that happened to cross her path.

Jake stepped away from the woman and removed a pen from his clipboard. "Good morning, ladies. You must be volunteers. I remember your faces but not the names. You are?"

"I'm Emma Cotton, and this is Kelly Grace. And, yes, we are here for our second day as volunteers." Not the sharpest pencil in the pack. The museum didn't have that many volunteers.

The woman brushed several locks of curly dark blond hair off her face with a gloved hand and extended the other to first Emma and then Kelly. "We've not met," she said. "I'm Claire Blevins. Let me know if I can answer any questions about the museum. I've worked here for years, since I was a volunteer in high school. Now I'm the assistant to Kayla Turner, the curator."

As Jake turned to greet other volunteers, the three women entered the building together. Then Kelly turned right toward the gift shop while Emma and Claire headed to the elevators.

"I'm sorry, I don't remember seeing you at the orientation or my first day last week," Emma said as soon as the elevator doors closed behind them.

"Don't be sorry," Claire replied. "I wasn't here. This is my first day back after having gallbladder surgery with some complications. I've been gone almost two months."

Emma let out a sigh of relief when the elevator stopped and the doors started to open. She never had liked elevators. She preferred to take the stairs when possible. "Kelly and I arrived for our first shift just as the security guard was escorting Ms. Nelson off the property after she was accused of stealing a painting." She cut her eyes at Claire. "That was a surprise."

Claire stepped off the elevator first and held the door as Emma followed. "I was shocked, to say the least, but I don't believe a word of it. Vanessa is a gossip, but she's good at her job and has always been trustworthy."

They walked down the hallway in the direction of the administrative suite. Emma wanted to pump as much information out of Claire as she could before they reached the offices. "Where was the painting last seen?"

Claire hesitated before answering. "I'm not sure exactly. But I was told that Kayla—the curator—verified it was ready for installation about two weeks ago. That would mean her initials are on the inventory form."

As they neared the offices, Emma felt her chances of learning more about Vanessa and her relationship with Claire slipping away. She stopped and looked Claire in the eyes. "Was anyone looking to take Vanessa's job? Did someone want her gone?"

Claire's blue eyes widened as her nostrils flared. "Are you insinuating something? I think you are getting involved in something that's none of your business. You are only a volunteer, after all. The museum board and security will handle the theft investigation. You have work to do."

Emma shook her head. Her heart sank. She'd pushed Claire too hard. "I'm sorry. I really didn't mean to imply anything. I … I'm sort of a mystery buff. I'm always asking questions." But Claire didn't hear the apology. She'd already disappeared behind the doors leading into the administrative suite.

Taking a minute to regain her composure, Emma straightened the bottom of her sweater over the hips of her slacks. She inhaled a deep breath, held it, and let the air trickle out through her lips. All was not lost. She had to keep a check on her emotions. Grabbing the strap of her shoulder bag with one hand, she pushed the door open with the other.

"Emma, good morning. Claire said you were on your way in." Marta Singh-Moon, the public relations director, stood in the doorway of her office and motioned Emma inside. "I have a project for you. Please, have a seat." Marta walked to the credenza behind her desk, picked up a spiral-bound book, and handed it to Emma. "We're updating our mailing and potential donor lists before it's time to mail our spring gala invitations. I need you to input the names and contact information for all of the entries in our guest book. It's easy but rather mind numbing, I'm afraid. I doubt it will take you too long. I tucked a note with the file name inside the guest book."

Opening the book, Emma looked at legible handwriting on Marta's note and hoped signatures in the book would be as easy to read. She flipped through the pages. "You're right. This shouldn't take too long. If there's nothing else, I'll get started."

"One more thing, Emma," Marta said. "Claire seemed out of sorts when she came in the office. She's a little on edge because she had a difficult time after her surgery. Just keep things light, OK?"

Emma searched Marta's face for camouflaged emotion but found none. "I understand."

"Good. Let me know if you have any questions. Ordinarily I'd let you work with Claire, but I think we'll give her time to handle her job reentry before working with a volunteer."

Emma was thankful to cross the aisle to her work space. If she remained quiet enough, maybe the staff would forget she was there and let something slip.

The office was quiet, though, and soon Emma was lost in her work with the same focus she had while working on intricate quilt restorations. Her fingers were as nimble on the computer keyboard as with a needle in fabric, and it didn't take long before she had turned several pages in the guest book. She'd flipped to a new page when her cellphone began vibrating in her purse. She pulled the phone from the side pocket. "Hello? Kelly?" Emma kept her voice low.

"Hold onto your hat, Emma. Our Dottie Faye is in the lobby creating quite the scene. The best I can tell, she's demanding a tour of the museum and yammering on about making a donation. And there's this strange bell-shaped thing hanging out of her purse." Kelly stopped to take a breath. "I think you'd better get down here."

Emma groaned. "Leave it to Dottie Faye to make a dazzling entrance. I guess this is what she meant yesterday when she said, 'I'll see you tomorrow.'" Emma saved the document on the computer and put Marta's slip of paper in the guest book to mark her spot. "I'll let Marta know I'm going downstairs for a bit, and then I'll be right there."

Emma's jaw dropped. Dottie Faye stood in the center of the lobby looking like she had teleported from the glitzy Southfork Ranch of the 1970s prime-time soap *Dallas*. A red designer suit dress hugged her figure, punctuated by a pair of red-and-black stilettos. A salt-and-pepper wig was pulled back into a French twist, and her unmistakably Southern accent now had a sophisticated air. Dottie Faye was clearly in prima donna mode.

"So you see, Mr. Jake and Miss Rita, I don't need to purchase a ticket because I intend to make a sizeable donation. An *impressively* sizeable donation." Dottie Faye did her best Southern belle smile for the security guard and cashier.

Rita, who had clearly been no match for Dottie Faye, was stammering an apology. Jake rested one hand on his gun holster and the other on Dottie Faye's arm. "Now, Mrs. Ewing, this is clearly a misunderstanding."

Emma stifled a giggled reaction to her aunt's alias, cleared her throat, and stepped through the crowd of people gathered by the reception desk. "Yes, it is a misunderstanding. This is my aunt, Dottie Faye. She wants to see the museum where I am volunteering and, based on a tour, possibly make a donation."

The crowd parted, and Marta walked to the small group standing in the middle of it. "Did I hear we have a potential donor here to take a tour? I'll be happy to give her a tour. You can all go back to work now," she said, nodding to Jake and Rita. She turned to Emma. "I'll take her by your desk at the end of the tour."

Kelly walked up to Emma as Dottie Faye and Marta approached the doorway of the first of several galleries. "Now if that doesn't beat everything. Dottie Faye decked out as Sue Ellen Ewing," Kelly said. "What's that thing sticking out of her bag?"

"That would be the SuperSleuther Conversation Magnifier, I think," Emma deadpanned.

Just as Emma and Kelly broke out in laughter, Dottie Faye turned, glanced at them over her shoulder, and winked.

"What do you think she is up to, anyway?" Kelly asked.

"Beats me," Emma replied. "I gave up trying to predict her behavior a long time ago. I know one thing: Marta will have her hands full for the next hour or so. Jake must have buzzed Marta at the same time you called me."

Kelly chuckled. "I expect Jake wasn't any more prepared to deal with Dottie Faye than poor Rita was."

"He does look a bit shell-shocked, doesn't he?" said Emma, glancing at her watch. "I need to get back to work. I had an interesting chat with Claire earlier. She was very defensive when I asked about Vanessa's job. But with Dottie Faye's diversion, who knows if I'll have the chance to find out anything else? I imagine her performance will be the talk of the museum today."

"No doubt," Kelly said. "I'd best get back to work too. I'll try to get the girls in the gift shop to talk about Claire. It won't be easy to get them off the topic of Dottie Faye, though. It sure didn't take our Dottie Faye long to attract their undivided attention."

Emma took the elevator to the third floor and returned to her work space in the administrative office suite. The office was quiet. Most of the staff and volunteers were still downstairs, likely discussing Dottie Faye's entertaining performance. Emma thought about seizing the opportunity to peek into Vanessa's office while everyone was distracted, but decided it would be best to complete at least some of her volunteer duties. It wouldn't be good if Marta began questioning her work ethic. Without conversations to distract her, it shouldn't take long to finish entering the guest book information into the computer.

She had typed in the last name and address when it suddenly hit her: Maybe the thief made an entry in the guest book. Even a fake name might provide a clue. Scrolling through the list of visitors, nothing really jumped out at her. Maybe she'd find something if she had time to really study the names. After standing up to take a quick glance around the room, Emma printed out the pages covering the last six weeks and sauntered across the suite to grab the document from the printer. She was back in her cubicle, stuffing the papers in her purse as Claire entered the suite.

"Your aunt is really something," said Claire, tossing her blond curls behind her shoulder. "Are you sure you're related?"

Emma wasn't quite sure how to respond. "Yes, she's something else. Dottie Faye never ceases to amaze me." Emma closed the guest book and clicked "Save" on the computer to store the new information she'd added to the potential donor list. "The morning has flown by. Marta and Dottie Faye should be finishing up their tour soon."

The door to the administrative offices opened and Dottie Faye's voice carried down the aisle of cubicles. "So this is where my Emma Jane volunteers. Where is she?"

"I'm right here, Dottie Faye," Emma said, raising her voice a bit so it would carry down the row of partitions but not disturb the employees and volunteers who had finally gotten back to work. She stepped into the aisle so Dottie Faye could easily find her.

"Emma Jane, this place is magnificent," said Dottie Faye, accenting every syllable as she tried to push the conversation magnifier farther into her purse. "I learned so much on the tour that Ms. Marta was kind enough to give me."

Emma looked at Marta and Jake, who had rounded the corner several paces behind Dottie Faye and were standing a respectful distance away. "Thanks for showing Dottie Faye around the museum. I really appreciate it."

Jake and Marta exchanged a silent look. Jake held out his arm. "Mrs. Ewing, I'm happy to accompany you to the front entrance. The twists and turns in this building can get quite confusing."

"Why thank you, young man," Dottie Faye said. "Just let me hug my Emma Jane goodbye."

She embraced Emma and spun her around so the two museum employees were blocked from view. "I have some useful information for you," Dottie Faye whispered. Emma could feel her aunt's breath on her ear.

Dottie Faye stepped back and turned to Jake and Marta. "Thank you again. I'm afraid I must get to another appointment." She glanced back at Emma. "I'll talk to you later, sugar. Call me."

"I'll do that," Emma said, exhaling a soft sigh when Dottie Faye started walking to the end of the line of cubicles. "Bye-bye."

ten

Emma and Kelly could hear the voices before they opened the door to Cotton & Grace.

"Oh no. My aunt and your mom are going at it again," Emma said, pushing on the door. "We really shouldn't allow them to be in the same room without a referee."

"Would you please go away and let me do this, you meddling old woman?" Maeve stood with her arms akimbo, staring at a quilt Dottie Faye was holding up to the wall behind the register. "I didn't tell you where to hang your half-naked valentine cherubs."

Dottie Faye tossed her head. "They weren't naked, and may I remind you that you're two years older than I am?"

Emma and Kelly listened silently for a moment before announcing their arrival. Emma cleared her throat. "What are you two up to now?"

The older women jumped slightly. Maeve grabbed the quilt from Dottie Faye and held it against her in a tight ball. "I wanted to surprise you with a St. Patrick's Day gift for the shop. But she came in before I could get it displayed properly."

Dottie Faye waved her hands in the air. "Well, she took down some of my Valentine's Day decorations and threw them aside."

Kelly put an arm around Dottie Faye. "Your Valentine's Day decorations were lovely and we all enjoyed them. But we always take them down before March first to get ready for St. Paddy's Day. Right, Emma?"

"Yes, that's true," Emma said. She gently took the quilt from Maeve's hands, shook it out, and held it up at arm's length. Celtic knot appliqués in green, black, and gold framed the edges. Inside was a single Celtic knot shamrock appliqué in varying green hues. "Oh, Maeve. It's absolutely gorgeous. What does this inscription on the tag mean?"

"It says *Lá Shona Fhéile Pádraig le Emma, mo treasured iníon-cara*. That means 'Happy St. Patrick's Day to Emma, my treasured daughter-friend.'" Maeve rubbed her finger over the tag. "I wanted to surprise you with something special this year."

"Oh, Dottie Faye," said Emma, turning to her aunt. "Isn't this beautiful?"

Dottie Faye nodded. "Yes, of course it is. Everything that woman makes is perfect." Her face softened. She looked first at Maeve and then to Emma. "It's obvious that she loves you very much."

"Thank you," Maeve said. "That's very kind of you to say."

Emma was pretty sure she had just heard the kindest words ever exchanged between her aunt and Kelly's mother. Were all of the planets aligned or something? She wondered if this could be the first step in a truce between the two warring women. But the thought disappeared as Dottie Faye pushed Maeve aside to grab her oversize purse from the register counter.

"You're welcome," said Dottie Faye. "Now, can we please focus on the information I gathered from my starring role at the museum this morning?"

Dottie Faye gestured to the chairs in the design alcove, her purse dangling from her elbow. "Let's sit down. Your museum people didn't make it easy on me this morning." She collapsed into a seat and wiped her brow. "That Marta person stuck to me like glue. She wasn't much for answering questions, either.

She droned on and on about dead artists and paintings that looked like they were painted by three-year-old children."

"So, what did you find out?" Emma asked.

"I had a lucky break when Helene somebody found us and asked Marta to go to her office and take a phone call. I very sweetly told Marta that was fine with me because then I'd have time to freshen up in the ladies' room," Dottie Faye said. "I excused myself and hid in the ladies' room a couple of minutes to make sure they had time to leave. Then I crept down the halls until I heard a conversation with my SuperSleuther Conversation Magnifier. I hit pay dirt outside the director's office. That Gabe Lucier and the curator, Kayla Turner, were debating whether or not Vanessa could have stolen the painting."

Dottie Faye paused for effect, patted her French twist, and clicked her nails on the arm of the chair.

Emma squirmed. "And?"

"Mr. Lucier said he trusted Vanessa, and that she was very good at her job. But Kayla Turner reminded him of her habit of spreading gossip and how it had gotten a friend in trouble." Dottie Faye sat back in her chair, obviously proud of the information she had to share.

"What friend? What trouble?" Emma was ready for some usable information.

"I don't know," Dottie Faye sighed. "But Mr. Lucier said a private detective was working on it. He hopes Vanessa isn't involved. Want to know what I think?"

"Oh, for heaven's sake, tell us," said Maeve. "We know you're going to anyway."

"I think this former co-worker or friend Vanessa had gotten in trouble set her up to take the fall for the stolen painting. It's a classic plot of greed and revenge," Dottie Faye said, moving her eyes from Emma to Kelly.

"Dottie Faye," Kelly said, catching Dottie Faye's eye, "Emma told me you mentioned having some useful information for us. Do you have more?"

Dottie Faye's grin almost lit up the alcove as she pulled a blue folder from her purse and handed it to Kelly with a flourish. "I sure do. Feast your eyes on this."

"I'll be darned. A copy of the new audit report," said Kelly, flipping quickly through the first few pages.

Emma stood and walked over to read the report over Kelly's shoulder. "Marta said it wasn't going to be released for a couple of weeks. How did you get a copy?"

"Oh, that was easy. I told them I wasn't opening my checkbook until my accountant examined their latest audit." Dottie Faye blew on the fingernails of her right hand and rubbed them on her shirt near the neckline. "Money really does talk, you know."

"Yes, you've obviously proven that," said Kelly as she looked up from the report. "This all looks like legalese to me. But Patrick is a whiz at deciphering these things because he compiles them all day. How about I take this home and let him take a peek at it? Maybe he will find another angle for us to consider."

Emma walked to the chart of suspects they'd hung in the storeroom and wrote "Vanessa's former friend/co-worker" on the list. "Well, this gives us another suspect to consider and a financial angle to study. Dottie Faye, your stint as Mrs. Ewing was a success, I'd say."

"Yes, it was. But now I must head to my nail appointment. I think I want glitter and rhinestones suitable for Mrs. Ewing," Dottie Faye said.

Maeve collected her purse and craft bag. "I'll walk you out. I have a few errands to run on the way home."

Emma and Kelly stared at the door as it closed behind Maeve and Dottie Faye.

"Do you suppose they'll scratch each other's eyes out before they reach their cars?" Kelly asked.

"That would be preferable to them hatching another plot to find me a husband," Emma replied.

Kelly nodded and snickered. "I think it's cute how they bond over your potential love life."

"You would," said Emma as she walked to the worktable. "But now we need to bond over the antique church quilt waiting to be restored. That woman from Mystic Harbor Community Church, Gloria Wetherell, is going to think we sent the quilt to China for restoration if we don't take time off from sleuthing to finish it."

They'd been working for about ten minutes when the shop bells jangled as Cammie Smythe, Kelly's new friend from the gift shop, and her mother, Catherine Hamilton, came through the door.

"What a quirky little building," Cammie said. She strode up to Kelly and Emma. "We love your shop. It's so cozy, isn't it, Mother?" Cammie ushered her mother to the design area and introduced her.

"It's very nice to meet you," Catherine said, holding out her hand first to Emma and then to Kelly. "My grandmother was a quilter, and I've been thinking of taking it up myself. Cammie suggested we stop by to see you while we were in Mystic Harbor."

Emma and Kelly welcomed Cammie and her mother into the shop. They gave the mother-daughter duo a quick rundown of their services, showed them various Cotton & Grace originals, and explained their current quilt restoration project. Cammie and Catherine took a lot of time perusing various items created by Emma and Kelly—hats, handbags, diaper totes, and even drink cozies.

"Your work is exquisite," said Cammie. "You both are so talented. I had no idea so many things were available in quilted forms."

Catherine ran her fingers over the bird-and-tree design of a baby quilt in bold primary colors. "I'd love to be able to make something like this for my grandchildren."

"You should check with Marcia Goode at Uncommon Threads about the quilting classes she offers. She has classes for all skill levels," said Emma.

Kelly nodded. "You two could take a class together. Quilting is a great mother-daughter activity. I have many fond memories of Mom teaching me the fundamentals."

Cammie laughed and her blue eyes twinkled beneath her black bangs. "I wish I had time to take a quilting class with her. Between the kids and my museum work, I don't have much time for anything else."

Emma saw her opening and took it. "How long have you been volunteering at the museum?"

"I started when my youngest started preschool. So that was about three years ago. I really love it," Cammie said.

"Our first day was rather exciting. We got here in time to see Vanessa escorted off the property. Rumors have been flying," said Kelly. "Do you know anything about Vanessa getting someone fired?"

Cammie closed her eyes in concentration. "I remember hearing some rumors after I started. Volunteers love to gossip. Rumor had it that a woman—I think her name was Devlin Williamson, or Williams—had quit her job at the Northeastern Museum of Art in Maine after Vanessa had spread gossip about her having a relationship with her boss.

I guess Vanessa had worked there before Boston Fine Arts. But that's all I know."

Elated to have a name to go on, but concerned Cammie would wonder why Kelly was so interested in Vanessa, Emma tried to hurry the conversation to an end. "I'm sorry we didn't have more of a chance to visit with Vanessa. During our orientation, she showed us the quilts in her office. She's gifted. I hope she's cleared of the theft. I'd love to see more of her work."

"I hope she's cleared before the newspapers get wind of the theft," Cammie said. "The museum doesn't need any bad publicity. Even with the economy improving, fundraising is still difficult. Donors get scared by scandal; it will keep them from contributing."

Catherine glanced at her watch. "Speaking of money, I need to get to the bank before it closes. But it was so nice to meet you. I'll definitely look into classes at Uncommon Threads. Thanks."

After seeing Cammie and her mother to the door, Emma and Kelly sank into the chairs in the alcove and considered the information Cammie had provided about Vanessa. Cammie had seemed certain of the first name of Vanessa's former co-worker and had offered enough of a clue to the last name to give them a starting point. But while Devlin wasn't a common name, both Williams and Williamson were.

Kelly glanced at the partially restored quilt on the worktable. "Emma, between volunteering on Mondays and running down clues, we've neglected the work that pays our bills. We don't have time to run down a name like Williams or Williamson. There could be thousands in New England, and she may not even live in the Northeast anymore."

Closing her eyes, Emma leaned her head back. Kelly was right. They needed help from someone more qualified than

Dottie Faye. But who? They certainly couldn't go to the police. "Know of any reputable private detectives?"

"No, but I know plenty of Irish cops in Boston. Dad had some friends in the department."

"Irish cops. Right. Somehow I don't think that's the direction we should take. Cops don't like me. I ask too many questions they can't answer. Need I remind you of the effect I have on Deputy Chief Boyer? I'd swear his blood pressure jumps twenty points when he looks at me. Do you have any other ideas?"

Kelly closed her eyes and sat quietly for a few seconds before opening them. "I guess we can check the Internet and see what we find. If one sounds promising, then we can ask for references."

"I'll grab my laptop and be right back. Thank goodness for Wi-Fi."

Emma and Kelly spent the next forty-five minutes searching online for detectives in the greater Boston-Mystic Harbor area. They were close to the top of the *Ms* in a listing on the Massachusetts Association of Private Detectives when they came across a familiar name.

"Alex Manning." Emma raised her eyebrows. "Didn't we go to high school with an Alex Manning? I think he was a senior when we were sophomores."

"Yep," Kelly said, nodding. "He was cute too, as I remember. Dark hair, green eyes, and not too tall for a shorty like me. Wasn't he in the Explorers program with the Mystic Harbor Police Department or something?"

Emma clicked on the link to Manning's credentials. "Well, there's no photo. But this Alex Manning retired from the New York City Police Department about two years ago and now owns Ace Investigations in Salem."

"Does he have a website?"

Emma's fingers flew over the computer keys. "Yep. It shows he provides all sorts of services—investigations ranging from asset searches and background checks to missing-person cases and surveillance. He does security consultation, he's a police procedure expert, and he provides references."

"I think you should call him, Emma. We don't have time to run down this Devlin person. We have people waiting on their quilts."

Emma fished her cellphone from her skirt pocket and dialed the number on Manning's website. She sighed when the call went to voice mail. She left her phone number and a message asking the detective to return her call.

"Now we can work on the quilt," she said, slipping the phone back into her pocket.

She turned on some light classical music and joined Kelly at the worktable to continue the quilt restoration project for the Mystic Harbor Community Church. The quilt had been made the same year the church was founded and had been presented to the first pastor. Emma felt like she was sewing herself into the history of Mystic Harbor as she stitched new life into the quilt.

Customer traffic was sparse, and the pair worked almost steadily for two hours, except when Kelly ran next door to Grounds for Suspicion to grab a quick snack. They were putting the quilt away and preparing to close the shop when Manning called.

"Alex Manning here. I'm returning your call."

When Emma asked if he was the Alex Manning who had attended Mystic Harbor High School, he confirmed he was one and the same. They reminisced about the year the football team won the state championship and the time his graduating class toilet-papered the principal's front yard.

"To date, I don't think any other class has had the guts to roll the principal's yard. Your class was a legend," Emma said.

"Yeah, we were. So, what can I do for you?"

She explained Vanessa's situation and told him Kelly was helping her clear the assistant curator's name. She didn't mention Rose. "We need you to find someone for us. A woman Vanessa knew several years ago. She seems to have disappeared off the map."

"Can you come by my office in the morning? I need to get more information from you and have you sign a contract."

"Let me check on something; hang on a moment, please." Emma placed her hand over the phone, motioning Kelly closer. "Can you go by to see Alex in the morning so I can meet with Gloria Wetherell about the Community Church quilt restoration?"

Kelly nodded.

"Alex, I have a meeting with a client in the morning, but Kelly can stop by on her way to the shop. Say, around nine thirty?"

"I'll see her then," Alex said, then cleared his throat. "And Emma, you need to keep in mind that sometimes bad things happen when people don't want to be found."

eleven

Alex Manning's ominous words still rang in Emma's ear as she unlocked the door to Cotton & Grace early the next day. She'd given up her morning run to devote a couple of extra hours to the Community Church quilt before Gloria Wetherell was due to arrive. Maybe she could make up for lost time before the shop opened. Kelly was right; the quilt was behind schedule. They couldn't risk their reputation of quality craftsmanship for the sake of Vanessa, even if she had promised information that might lead them to Rose's killer.

As Emma gathered the quilt, quilt log, and her supplies, she wondered what Alex would tell Kelly at their meeting. Alex's words, "Bad things happen when people don't want to be found," echoed in her mind. *What kinds of things? Were you giving us a warning?* Her thoughts faded as she spread the quilt on the table with care. As always, she felt the stress melt away as she became immersed in the story of the quilt and wondered about the generations of people it had kept warm. Gloria said it had been a gift to the church's first pastor nearly two hundred years ago, which is why she wanted it restored for the church's bicentennial celebration.

It was a beautiful, well-used old quilt. While tips of the eight-point stars had come loose and a number of seams along the triangles in the Irish chain pattern had frayed, somehow the detailed floral and plaid designs had retained much of their color—Turkey red, Prussian blue, and early green. Working from top to bottom, Emma and Kelly had begun to carefully restitch areas where the fabric had come loose and replace the material that was torn or missing with a similar reproduction. They were about half finished with the restoration, so Gloria would have a good sense of the "before and after" look of the quilt.

Three sharp raps on the shop door broke the silence and Emma glanced at the clock. Was it really nine thirty already? She hurried to the door, flipped the sign to "Open," and unlocked the door. Gloria was right on schedule.

"Good morning, Gloria. I was working on the church quilt. It's coming along nicely," Emma said, holding the door ajar as the older, gray-haired woman stepped inside.

"I can't wait to see it. The bicentennial committee members are very excited about putting it on display at the celebration."

Emma raised her arm in the direction of the worktable. "Come take a peek at it, but keep in mind that we're only about halfway done. Quilt restoration takes time when done properly."

Waddling into the alcove, Gloria clapped her hands together when she saw the quilt. "It's beautiful already. Half done, you say? Will you have time to complete it?"

"Yes, we'll have it done in time," said Emma. *We will if we can solve the painting theft fast enough.*

Gloria *oohed* and *aahed* over the quilt for about ten minutes until Maeve's arrival, with a box of St. Patrick's Day decorations, seemed to distract her. After a slight hesitation, she greeted Maeve, pulled a small camera out of her purse, and snapped a photo of the quilt. "It looks like you have things to do, and I need to stop by the church to check on the historical display," Gloria said, slipping the camera back into her purse. "I'll check in with you next week."

After the door had closed behind Gloria, Emma let out a sigh of relief. "I'm thankful she didn't seem too concerned that the quilt isn't even close to being finished."

"You've been a bit distracted lately between trying to solve all of the mysteries that keep popping up," Maeve said. "I'm sure Dottie Faye's matchmaking complicates things too." Maeve removed a small statue of St. Patrick, a ceramic plaque of an Irish blessing, and two Irish throw blankets from the box. "Emma, I apologize for my part in Dottie Faye's scheme at the ball. My nephew Aidan is such a nice young man, and I think the world of you. When Dottie Faye mentioned getting you tickets to the ball, I thought it might be fun for you and Aidan to reconnect. I didn't mean to interfere. I want you to enjoy life."

Emma took Maeve's hand. "I know you both meant well, but I *do* enjoy life." She gazed at Maeve's quilt of shamrocks and Celtic knots hanging behind the register. She knew Maeve considered her a second daughter. "I will say I'm not sure which amuses me less—the thought of you and Dottie Faye as co-conspirators in running my love life or the constant bickering between the two of you."

"I'll try to stay out of your love life," said Maeve, giving Emma a hug, "but I can't promise the bickering will stop anytime soon."

"I'll take what I can get." Emma stepped back a bit when the shop door opened.

"Emma Jane, what is going on here?" Dottie Faye's stilettos clicked on the wood floor. She sashayed to the register counter as Maeve unboxed the rest of the St. Patrick's Day decorations.

"Nothing is 'going on,' Dottie Faye. Maeve and I were catching up. That's all."

"And redecorating, I see." Dottie Faye tapped the pointy toe of one rhinestone-studded shoe and crossed her arms.

Emma figured she'd better give her aunt a hug too. She draped an arm across the back of Dottie Faye's shoulders and squeezed. "I love your Valentine's Day decorations. I enjoy them every year. But it's time to start thinking about St. Patrick's Day."

"OK. I get it. I'll get my box from the back room and pack up the rest of Cupid's things, especially since Maeve already started moving them." Dottie Faye's bottom lip curved into a pout before she disappeared into the storeroom.

Dottie Faye had just reappeared when Kelly pushed open the front door with a bag of pastries from The Chocolate Cauldron in one hand and a notepad in the other. "Good. You're all here. Now I'll only have to go through this once."

"What, no coffee?" Emma said. "You slacker."

"I figured you had your two cups by now."

"You're right. I have," said Emma. "So, what else do you have for us?"

The women settled in the alcove with Maeve and Dottie Faye in the two overstuffed chairs and Kelly and Emma sitting at the worktable. The pastry bag remained on the register counter.

Kelly looked at Dottie Faye. "First, you'll be pleased to know that Alex Manning is still ruggedly handsome. He doesn't smile much though."

"OK, what else?" Emma was anxious to prevent any comments about her love life.

"Not so fast, Emma Jane. Who is this ruggedly handsome Alex Manning, and is he an eligible bachelor?" Dottie Faye bounced her gaze from Emma to Kelly. "And why haven't I heard of him before now?"

"Alex Manning? The star athlete of your high school?" Maeve grinned at Dottie Faye, clearly pleased to have information her adversary didn't. "All of the girls had crushes on him back then, even our Rose."

Emma took a deep breath and tried to contain her impatience. "He's all grown up now and is a retired cop. Alex owns

Ace Investigations in Salem, and we've hired him to find the woman who supposedly lost her job because of Vanessa's gossip," Emma said. "I don't know if he's single, but can we please let Kelly tell us what she learned during her meeting with him?"

"He asked me all sorts of questions about Vanessa and Devlin," Kelly said. "I didn't know the answer to a lot of them. He wanted to know why we were helping Vanessa. I told him she was Rose's friend a long time ago, and she'd asked us to help. Then I signed a contract and paid him a small advance. That's all. He said he should have something to tell us in twenty-four hours or so."

"So, I guess we wait," Emma said. "This will give us some time to work on the church quilt. Gloria was pleased with the work so far and didn't seem too worried about it being done in time for the celebration—although she did ask about it. I don't like cutting it so close."

Maeve stood up and smoothed the bottom of her beige cowl-neck shirt over the hips of her navy slacks and turned toward the counter. "I'm going to get started on the St. Patrick's Day decorations. Don't mind me. I'll work around you."

When Dottie Faye rose and followed Maeve, Emma braced for the bickering. But she was surprised. Her aunt hummed what Emma thought might be a Hank Williams song and packed up her Valentine's Day trappings without swapping barbs with Kelly's mom.

Emma resumed work on the church quilt and was soon joined by Kelly when the pastries were gone.

"What time did you get here this morning?" Kelly asked. "You really made some headway. This pinwheel block looks almost as good as new," she said, examining the work Emma had completed.

Before Emma could answer, her cellphone chimed from the table beside her. She picked it up and glanced at the caller ID. *Why is Eric Hart calling?*

"Hello, Eric?" Emma said tentatively. "How are you?"

"Emma, good morning. I'm great. Thanks. I had two patients cancel at the last minute and wondered if you had time to grab that cup of coffee we discussed at the hospital ball."

"Coffee? Right now?" Emma hesitated until Kelly gave her arm a playful slap, nodded and silently mouthed, "Go."

"Yes," Eric replied. "I can be at your shop in about five minutes."

"All right. I'll see you then," Emma stammered. "Goodbye."

In the time it took for Eric to say "bye" and for Emma to hang up the phone, Kelly, Maeve, and Dottie Faye descended upon her. She held a hand up in warning. "Don't say a single word. It's just coffee."

Kelly grinned, rolling her eyes. "We don't have to say a word. You already know what we're thinking."

Emma gathered her purse and coat and waited by the door for Eric to arrive. She didn't want him to be subjected to comments from the peanut gallery, no matter how well intentioned. As he approached, she opened the door and left the chuckling trio behind her.

"Emma," Eric said as he stepped onto the curb in front of the shop. "It's great to see you. Normally I get irritated when patients cancel last-minute, but today it was a godsend."

Emma wasn't quite sure what to say. She paused and watched the warmth of Eric's breath meet the cold, sending vapor into the air. "I got to work two hours early today, so I was ready for a break," Emma said.

Squeezing past Eric as he held the door to the coffee shop open, Emma was mortified when her elbow brushed across his side. She looked up at him to apologize and felt her pulse quicken when his brown eyes stared back at her. What was wrong with her? "Wow, there are a lot of people in here," she said, quickly scanning the room. "There's a table in the back corner."

Eric suggested Emma grab the table while he placed their order. She agreed and started to dig the wallet out of her purse. "No, this is on me," he said. "How do you like your coffee?"

"A splash of cream only. And thanks."

"So you're sweet enough without sugar, is that what you're saying?" Eric said with a mischievous grin.

A nervous laugh escaped Emma's lips, so she pointed toward the corner. "I'll go and get our table before someone else does."

She busied herself with checking email on her smartphone while awaiting Eric's arrival with their coffee. By the time Eric sat in the chair opposite Emma, she'd read a chatty email from her father, who was enjoying retired life in Florida.

"One black coffee with a splash of cream," Eric said, setting down a tray laden with two steaming mugs of coffee and a plate of four round cake bites. "I grabbed us a little snack too."

Holding the heavy blue mug in both hands, Emma closed her eyes and inhaled the aroma. "Mmm—this smells good. It's just what I need after a long morning. I came in early to work on a quilt restoration that's a little behind schedule."

"Dottie Faye told me you're also volunteering at the art museum. Between running your business, volunteer work, and amateur sleuthing, you must stay pretty busy. My life pales in comparison." He held up the plate for Emma to take a cake bite. "How's the quest to find Rose's killer?"

Emma popped the bite into her mouth and washed it down with a swig of coffee. "Actually, the art museum is part of the investigation, although the people there don't know that, so please keep it to yourself," she said. "We'll find Rose's killer; I know we will."

"I expect so," said Eric as he picked up a cake bite and dunked it quickly in his coffee. "From what I see, tenacity runs in your family."

Emma didn't want to discuss Dottie Faye and her obvious matchmaking, so she steered the conversation toward Riley and the challenges Eric had as a single father. Although she had no children of her own, she enjoyed hearing his heartwarming stories of his ten-year-old daughter. The time passed quickly, and Emma was a bit disappointed when Eric's receptionist called to say a sick patient had phoned, begging to be worked in as soon as possible.

"I wish I didn't have to leave, but duty calls," he said. "Thank you for meeting me on such short notice."

"I understand. Work awaits me too." Emma stood and slipped on her jacket. "Thanks for the coffee."

They said a quick goodbye outside Cotton & Grace. When Emma walked in the door, Kelly was waiting for her.

"The coast is clear. I'm the only one here. How did it go?" Kelly sounded almost as hopeful as Dottie Faye. Almost.

Emma took off her coat and hung it on the peg behind the register. "We talked about Rose and the investigation until I changed the subject and asked about Riley. Boy, he adores that little girl. He beams when he talks about her. I must admit that he is attractive."

"Don't let Dottie Faye hear you say that. She'll be planning your wedding," Kelly said.

"Perish the thought," Emma replied with a shudder. "On a nicer note, Maeve did a beautiful job on the St. Patrick's Day decorations. The quilt she made me is gorgeous."

"Speaking of Mom, at this very moment she is at my

house fixing dinner, and you're invited. Patrick called while you were gone and said he found something very interesting with the audit. He didn't give any details, but he hinted that Claire Blevins may not be as innocent as everyone thinks."

Emma glanced at the clock. It was a little after noon. "That must be some dinner your mom is fixing."

"Well, the fact that you'll be at the table must've inspired her. She'll come up with something special for you."

"I'm sure she will," Emma said. "In the meantime, maybe we can get a few hours of work done on the church quilt."

They worked steadily all afternoon with few interruptions, save a couple of phone inquiries and Kelly's quick trip next door to tame her voracious appetite. Emma found the intricate work relaxing, not only because the required concentration took her mind off Rose. It was a relief to be making headway on the quilt. They accomplished more when they worked together, despite Kelly's need for frequent breaks to release extra energy. Emma wondered if Kelly's fidgeting could be a result of all the sugar she ingested over the course of a day.

The sun had already set when Emma and Kelly began packing up the quilt supplies. As they began shutting down the shop for the day, Alex Manning called Emma's cellphone with information about Devlin. Emma put him on speakerphone and placed the phone on the register counter. "Alex, Kelly's here with me, and we have you on speakerphone."

"Great." Alex skipped the pleasantries and got right down to business. "You're looking for a Devlin Williamson, that much I know. I discovered the Northeastern Museum of Art receives government funding, so I made a public records request for the personnel files of all employees or former employees with the first or middle name Devlin and the last name of Williams or Williamson. These records confirmed her name. I can't find any updated information on her. She seems to have dropped off the planet." He paused and Emma could hear him flipping through his notes. "But I did find the name and address of her mother, a Ruth Williamson, listed on the employment application as an emergency contact. She lives in a house in Salem that is—get this—supposedly haunted."

"Haunted, huh? Yeah, OK." Emma grabbed a pen and paper and jotted down the woman's name, address, and phone number. "Did you contact her?"

"No, I didn't want to spook her," he deadpanned.

Kelly chuckled. "Oh, so you've developed a sense of humor since high school."

"A little, but it can be our secret. Do you want me to contact Ruth Williamson for you?"

Emma looked at Kelly and hesitated for a moment. It was tempting. "No, I think we'll try first. If we have issues, then we'll give you a call."

"Sounds good. I'll wait to hear from you. *Ciao.*"

Staring down at her notes, Emma was relieved to have a next step. "So, how does this Saturday sound for a trip to Salem?"

"That'll work. Mom can watch the shop. Most likely she'll be here tweaking her decorations anyway." Kelly donned her jacket and flipped off all of the lights except the one they kept on for security purposes.

Emma slipped her notes into her purse and shrugged into her coat. "I can't quite figure out how an outsider would have the means and opportunity to steal the painting, but I guess anything's possible."

She stood by as Kelly turned on the alarm. They had installed it after their investigation into Rose's death had resulted in several break-ins. The street was cold and quiet as they turned toward their cars. The silence was broken when a sudden gust of wind whirled down the sidewalk and knocked the shop's sign off its hinges, sending it crashing to the ground.

'Tis an ill wind that blows no good, Emma thought.

twelve

"Look who I found when I was taking out the trash," Patrick said as he held open the swinging kitchen door for Emma to pass before he retreated to the living room.

"After all these years, am I now discovering you're a dumpster diver?" Kelly quipped as she turned from the cupboard with a stack of soup bowls in her hand. "What took you so long, anyway? Did you dive in several dumpsters along the way?"

"Very funny. I see you're perfecting your George Burns–and–Gracie Allen routine." Emma said. "I took a bit longer to get here because I stopped by Wiley Howard's sign shop on the way to see if he can fix our sign. When I showed him the damage, he asked what had happened to it. I made the mistake of telling him the truth and he proceeded to expound upon the legendary perils that befall shopkeepers when their signs fall off their hinges."

Maeve groaned. "That old man is a brilliant craftsman, but he has more superstitions than Boston has Irish, and that's saying something, coming from a woman who grew up listening to Celtic lore and tales of the Salem witch trials."

Emma lifted the lid of a giant Dutch oven sitting on the stove and inhaled deeply. "Lamb stew. My favorite."

"She even made wheaten bread just for you," Kelly said, placing the bowls next to the stove. "You need to come to dinner more often. I love having Mom in my kitchen."

"My taste buds would love the break from the steady diet of frozen dinners, but I fear my waistline would revolt." Emma loved the nostalgia of the refrigerator magnets still holding up childhood artwork of Kelly's now college-age children, Keith and Julie. Each of the four white chairs around the small pine table had a green-stenciled name surrounded by burgundy hearts. Kelly had stenciled the chairs to match the hearts-and-cottage design she'd put on the walls. Emma knew Kelly had spent many hours supervising homework and art projects here. There was love in this kitchen.

Maeve handed Emma a basket crammed with bread. "Would you please set this on the dining room table and ask Patrick to come in here? Everything else is ready to go. We'll serve the stew from the stove."

In short order, the four were seated around the table with steaming bowls of stew before them. Emma didn't waste any time steering the conversation toward the museum's financial situation. "Patrick, Kelly said you found information in the audit that might have some bearing on Vanessa's case."

Patrick fished a piece of bread from the basket and asked Kelly to pass the butter. He spoke while meticulously spreading butter on one side of the slice. "It looks like the museum is floundering. Its bottom line is in the red for the fourth year in a row. The recession has been tough on everyone, especially nonprofits. Donors don't have the dollars to contribute these days."

Patrick paused and took a bite of bread. He looked pensive as he chewed, and Emma wondered what was going on in his head.

He took a swallow of water and wiped his mouth with a napkin. "I trust this won't leave this room because we are all a family here," he said, looking Emma in the eye.

"Agreed." Emma leaned forward in her chair, her spoon perched in midair. "Go on."

"I called a friend of mine who is a CPA at the firm that completed the audit and asked a few questions. He said the auditor suggested cutting several positions, and one of them was the administrative assistant to the curator." He looked across the table at Emma. "I thought that was significant."

Emma put her spoon in the bowl and rested against the back of her chair. "That gives Claire a motive. Maybe Claire had the painting stolen during Vanessa's watch so she'd be fired. Then Claire could step into the assistant curator position. It's the promotion she's been hoping for since finishing her degree."

"Maybe we need to look at the board members," Kelly said. "Or the director. One of them may have stolen it so the museum could collect the insurance money to bolster its financial position."

"That scenario is unlikely," Patrick said, shaking his head. "An investigation by an insurance company would alert the press and possibly end up in the newspapers. The museum board wouldn't want that. I suspect the fear of negative publicity is why the investigation is being done in-house."

When all four bowls and the breadbasket were empty, Maeve cleared the table and sliced the potato cake onto plates while Patrick showed Emma and Kelly proof of the museum's failing finances. Emma hardly noticed when Maeve placed the cake in front of her. She was too engrossed in Patrick's explanation of the audit and his review of the auditor's comments. He left no doubt in Emma's mind—something was amiss at the Boston Fine Arts Museum.

Maeve spoke when there was a lull in the conversation. "It isn't too late to call Vanessa and see if you could visit with her tonight. Now that you have some facts and figures, maybe she will have something else to say."

Kelly looked at Emma. "I'm game if you are."

"That works for me. Maybe the traffic won't be so bad at this hour," Emma said.

While everyone else dug into the cake, Emma dialed Vanessa's number. The phone conversation lasted less than a minute. "She said she'd see us in an hour. I guess she's as anxious as we are to get this mystery solved," Emma said.

"Yes! I not only got out of cooking, but now I miss the cleanup too." Kelly gave her mom a hug. "Make sure Patrick helps too. He knows his way around the kitchen."

Patrick grabbed a towel and playfully popped Kelly on the shoulder with it. "Thanks for telling all of my secrets," he teased. "But seriously, you're getting into some seamy stuff here. Please be careful, both of you."

"We're always careful. We know to not go popping people with towels." Kelly stood on her tiptoes and kissed him on the cheek. "You worry too much."

Emma thanked Patrick for his help and hugged Maeve to show appreciation for the dinner. "Don't worry. I'll keep her out of trouble."

"And that's supposed to make us feel better?" Patrick laughed. "Now, go on and get this done before it gets too late."

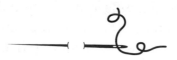

Emma drummed her fingers lightly on the steering wheel of the Jeep as she drove toward Boston. "Patrick sure has a good sense of humor for an accountant. I've never seen him pop you with a towel before. Does he do that often?"

"I'll never tell." Kelly grinned. "I think he's enjoying helping us with the museum mystery. I always keep him updated on our quest to find out who killed Rose, but he doesn't often get to be involved with the investigations."

"Maybe we'll find the killer faster if we include him more," Emma said.

"Maybe. We may need his financial expertise again at some point before we get to the bottom of Rose's murder."

They spent most of the drive deciding who was going to ask Vanessa which questions. First, they'd show her the audit and study her reaction. Then they'd ask her about Claire and the possibility of the administrative assistant setting Vanessa up for the theft. By the time Emma had exited off the interstate and driven several blocks to Vanessa's street, they had it all planned.

"I think we're getting closer to solving this," Kelly said while digging around in Emma's CD case.

"Umm, maybe not," Emma said. "Look ahead."

"What in the world? Flashing lights, emergency vehicles, and lots of smoke. It looks like Doomsday." Kelly slid a U2 CD into the stereo but turned down the volume.

Emma groaned and brought her fist down on the steering wheel. "It looks like we won't be getting anywhere near Vanessa's apartment."

She turned down the only road not blocked by the police and fire departments and circled back to the interstate while Kelly called Vanessa. Emma tried to keep up with Kelly's side of the conversation, but there were too many distractions with the emergency vehicles and traffic jam. She gave up and focused on the road.

"Well?" Emma said when Kelly hung up the phone.

"Vanessa said the fire is across the street and three doors down. She's safe and people in her building have not been asked to evacuate." Kelly slipped her phone into her purse. "She offered to come by the shop tomorrow. I told her to stop by anytime because we'd be there all day. Wednesdays are usually slow, so I thought we'd have time to talk."

As Emma merged into the traffic on the freeway, her mind was whirling. She didn't have any doubt they'd eventually find out who killed Rose, but she was getting tired of setbacks. Was it terrible that she was more concerned about the delay in the investigation than the safety of the residents on Vanessa's street?

"Kelly, do you ever worry about not finding Rose's killer?"

"Never."

"Good. Me neither. I wish it'd happen sooner than later."

Emma was so engrossed in reading an online newspaper story about the fire that she didn't hear the shop bells when Vanessa came through the door the next morning. She nearly slid off the stool behind the register when the suspected art thief leaned over and said a sharp, "Good morning."

"Vanessa. Hello." Emma stood up and wiggled her nose as the aroma of Chanel No. 5 wafted over the counter. "I was reading about the fire. I'm relieved nobody was hurt."

Emma felt a little frumpy in what had become her normal work attire—sweater, longish skirt, and sensible shoes—next to Vanessa, who wore a designer power suit and high heels. The woman might be temporarily out of work, but you'd never know it by the way she dressed.

"Yes, no one was hurt. It's a mess on our block and congested in the surrounding area. I had to walk quite a way to reach a place where my friend could pick me up to drive me here," Vanessa said. "Now I'm here, so what is the information you have about the theft?"

"I'd rather wait until Kelly gets back. She went to the office supply store. We ran out of printer paper this morning," Emma said. "She'll be back soon."

Vanessa strolled around the shop and paused to look at the display of items designed by Emma and Kelly. She glanced at the variety of electronic tablet sleeves, teapot cozies, cases for eyeglasses, and purses, but seemed particularly interested in the wall hangings, lap quilts, and seasonal door panels. "You have an eye for design. I found a copy of your book, but it doesn't do justice to your work," she said, studying the stitching on a spring wall hanging featuring an impressionistic design of blue raindrops and pastel spring flowers. "Rose would be very proud of you."

"Rose was so far ahead of her time as a fiber artist, there's no telling where she'd be now if she hadn't fallen down those stairs." Emma said. She watched Vanessa's eyes narrow and wondered what that meant. "It's hard to believe she was only twenty-six years old."

"Indeed," said Vanessa.

She'd not taken the bait, and Emma was perplexed by the incongruous combination of Vanessa's obvious affection for Rose's memory and her calculated use of information surrounding her death, which bordered on extortion.

Emma was about to try another tactic when Kelly came bounding through the door with several reams of printer paper.

"I wanted to make sure we wouln't run out of paper any time soon," Kelly said, walking straight toward the printer. "Oh—hi, Vanessa. How are you after last night's excitement?"

"Somewhat tired, but mostly curious about what you seemed so anxious to talk about last night that you drove into Boston to see me." She placed a hand on her hip. "So, what is it?"

"Why don't you sit down? We have something to show you." Emma grabbed the museum's audit from the register counter and joined Vanessa and Kelly in the alcove. "Have you seen the museum's new audit report?"

Vanessa reached out to retrieve the document from Emma's outstretched hand. "How did you get a copy? I hadn't even gotten one before I was so unceremoniously escorted out of the building."

"We could tell you—but then we'd have to kill you," said Kelly, doing her best humorous spy imitation.

"Ahem, well, don't mind her," said Emma when Vanessa's face darkened. "She's seen too many espionage movies on television while fighting the empty-nest syndrome."

Kelly apologized for her choice of words. "I'm sorry. I shouldn't have made such a tasteless joke under the circumstances. My weird sense of humor gets the best of me sometimes. We wanted to talk to you about the museum's cash flow, and we wondered if it could be motivation for the theft."

"I'd heard talk of cutbacks," Vanessa said, glancing through the audit booklet. "But Kayla Turner, my boss, assured me that my job wasn't in jeopardy. I hope you're not insinuating that I stole the painting."

"Not at all," said Emma, hoping to prevent Vanessa from becoming even more defensive. "We're trying to come up with a list of other suspects."

The shop phone rang, cutting the uneasy silence. Emma excused herself and walked to the register counter to answer it. As the caller droned on about wanting to take a quilting class, Emma watched the two women in the alcove sit silently; she was surprised her usually chatty friend was so quiet. When the caller finally took a breath, Emma suggested she call Marcia at Uncommon Threads and recited the number to her.

Just as Emma returned to the alcove, Kelly glanced up at her and started talking. "Vanessa, we heard a rumor that Claire's job as assistant-to-the-curator was on the chopping block. We were also told that Claire Blevins has been after your job for a long time, especially since completing her master's degree."

"This gives Claire a motive for stealing the painting," Emma said, trying to choose her next words carefully. "Maybe Claire set you up to be blamed for the theft. You'd be fired and she could get your job."

"You two have quite the imagination. The idea of Claire stealing the painting and taking my job is ludicrous. I trained Claire to eventually take over as assistant curator."

She jumped from the chair and paced back and forth across the alcove, obviously debating whether or not to say what was on her mind. Emma thought it best to keep quiet until Vanessa had made her decision. She prayed Kelly was thinking the same thing. They didn't have to wait long.

"It's not common knowledge, so please don't spread this around the museum, but I'll be leaving soon to take over as curator of a museum in Chicago. I'd recommended Claire for the assistant curator position when she had emergency surgery." Vanessa returned to her seat and crossed her legs. "I didn't want to tell you about it, but I guess I have to trust you since you're trying to clear my name."

Emma nodded. "We know about Devlin Williamson. We overheard two staff members talking about her. Evidently she was pretty hot about losing her job. The word on the street is that you spread gossip about her affair with her boss. Could she be responsible for the theft?"

Looking contrite for the first time since Emma had met her, Vanessa closed her eyes and bowed her head for a moment before answering. "I'll always regret doing something so stupid and spiteful. It really wasn't about Devlin at all. My fiancé had broken off our engagement weeks before the wedding, and I guess I wanted someone else to hurt as much as I did. A year or so later, I tried to make amends by writing her a letter of apology. I never received a reply, not that I blame her. I have no idea where she is now."

"Could she be responsible for the theft?" Emma repeated.

Vanessa shook her head. "No, I don't think so. She is probably more hurt than angry with me. Devlin is basically a good person, or she was when I worked with her. She was quiet and unassuming, and she minded her own business."

Kelly stood up and held her hand out to Vanessa. "Thanks for sharing that with us."

Emma shook Vanessa's hand too. "We promise to let you know as soon as we find out anything else."

Emma and Kelly didn't say anything else until Vanessa had stepped onto the sidewalk and the door had closed behind her.

"We still can't cross Claire's name off the list, no matter what Vanessa says," Kelly said.

"Nope. And don't forget our Saturday-morning jaunt to Salem to find Devlin Williamson."

Kelly chuckled. "You still have that uncanny ability to read my mind."

By the time Emma laced up her running shoes, she was a bundle of nervous energy. The church quilt still wasn't done, even though they'd worked on it all afternoon after Vanessa's visit. While Vanessa seemed to think neither Claire nor Devlin would have set her up, Emma still thought one of them could be the thief. She couldn't cross anything off her to-do list, and that was irritating.

The sun had already slipped below the horizon as Emma set out on her run wearing a jacket with reflective bands and a flashlight. She'd lived in her little cottage for years and her feet seemed to follow the road with little input needed from her brain. That was good because she had a lot on her mind between finishing the church quilt restoration, clearing Vanessa, and solving Rose's murder. The only thing that relaxed her mind as much as running was quilting, and she loved doing both. She'd developed several running routes through the streets of Mystic Harbor and chose her course depending upon the time she had and the number of problems she needed to solve. Tonight she chose the five-mile run.

Emma noticed the dark sedan as she was completing the second mile. It caught her attention only because it came perilously close to the side of the road and she was forced to jump the curb to keep it from hitting her. She shined her flashlight directly in its path and chalked the incident up to a distracted driver. She saw it the second time around mile four as she passed Pastor Goodman's house on Fallen Street, a name she found hopelessly ironic.

When the car made a third appearance, she decided to tack on a couple of extra miles and take a new route to zigzag through the neighborhood. She didn't believe in coincidences. Nor did she see any sense in pushing her luck. It took her twenty minutes longer to return to the cottage, and she still felt like someone was watching her as she unlocked her front door. "Get a grip, Emma. Your mind is playing tricks on you," she said aloud, partly to test her voice and partly to announce her entrance to anyone who might be waiting inside.

thirteen

Emma glanced in her rearview mirror and started backing the Jeep down the driveway when Dottie Faye pulled up in her Caddy, blowing the horn and blocking the exit.

She jumped out of the Jeep to see her aunt with the driver's-side window down despite the chilly air. "Dottie Faye! Stop blowing your horn. We have neighbors who sleep late on Saturday mornings."

"I am not missing your trip to Salem," said Dottie Faye. "Now be a love and move your car so I can park mine in the driveway."

Once the cars were jockeyed into position, Dottie Faye grabbed a large bag out of the Caddy, threw it into the backseat of the Jeep, and climbed in the passenger side.

"Whatcha have there?" Emma asked after the door slammed.

"I brought my new EVP recorder and EMF reader along with the other ghost-hunting equipment I bought on special," Dottie Faye replied. "You said this woman's house is haunted."

"No, I said people say it's haunted. That's not the same thing." Emma looked in the backseat and rolled her eyes at the huge duffel bag filled with bulky gizmos. "Dottie Faye, why do you waste your money on that useless stuff?"

Dottie Faye stuck out her lower lip. "It's not useless. Besides, ever since I moved here, I've heard about the witch trials and ghosts in Salem. But I haven't seen anything that can compete with the voodoo curses down in Mississippi. I have Southern bragging rights to protect here."

Dottie Faye rambled on about her ghost-hunting equipment during the ten-minute drive to the Grace home. Emma
was grateful for the distraction when Kelly power-walked down
her brick driveway and jumped into the backseat. She groaned
when the duffel bag became a topic of conversation.

"What do we have here, a leprechaun carrier?" Kelly slapped
the top of the duffel bag and chortled.

Emma cast a disapproving glance into the rearview mirror.
"Don't encourage her, please."

"Emma Jane, I really wish you'd not talk about me as if
I wasn't here," Dottie Faye said, leaning over to place a hand
on Emma's shoulder. "It's not polite."

"I'd like you to keep in mind that we are going to Salem
to talk with Devlin Williamson's mother. We're *not* hunting
paranormal beings conjured by your imagination. This trip is
serious."

"It's not my imagination. The Williamson house is listed
on Salem's Haunted Places Registry. I brought my equipment
along so I can check it out for myself. Don't worry about me. I
won't get in the way. You have your investigation, and I have
mine."

Kelly leaned forward in her seat. "I hope Mrs. Williamson
isn't too shocked to see us, especially when you lug in all this
equipment, Dottie Faye."

"You mean she doesn't know we're coming?"

"Well, no—" Kelly hesitated.

"We wanted the element of surprise," Emma interjected.

Emma slid a CD into the player and the sound of Charlie
Daniels's fiddle filled the car. Soon Dottie Faye's silly ghost
rambling would cease. Her aunt couldn't resist Southern rock.
It wouldn't be long before her head of teased blond hair was
bouncing to the music. Emma's wait was short. By the time

the first strains of Lynyrd Skynyrd's contribution to the *Super Southern Rock* CD started, Dottie Faye was holding an imaginary microphone. Mission accomplished.

The CD was starting over when Emma, following the advice of the GPS navigation system on Kelly's smartphone, turned down a tree-lined street of old but mostly well-maintained homes. "This is the block. We're almost there. It's number 607." She drove slowly, glancing from side to side at the houses.

"It's this one," said Dottie Faye, her voice tinged with excitement and curiosity.

Emma tried to imagine what the home had looked like before it became something suitable for a set in a Tim Burton movie. Her imagination wasn't that good. Streaks of grime fell from each of the twelve windows—three rows of four each—looking like tears rolling down the side of an unkempt face. Overgrown hedges blocked some of the walkway and partially obscured the bottom row of windows.

Emma pulled to the curb and gazed at the house. It sure wasn't what she had expected. If she didn't know better, she'd wonder if Dottie Faye hadn't set the whole thing up.

She double-checked the address on the house and compared it to the sticky note she'd placed on the dashboard just to make sure the GPS had not led them astray. It was the right place all right. But could someone actually live here? Was it safe to go in?

"And you said it wasn't haunted. I sure am glad I brought my ghost-hunting gear. I think I'm going to need it."

"Are those vines growing out of the gable roof over the door?" Emma asked in disbelief. "Am I seeing that right?"

"Yep, those would be vines strangling the house," Kelly said. "I'm waiting for a horror movie character to peek out of a top-floor window."

Dottie Faye heaved the duffel bag onto her lap and put her hand on the door handle. "Oh, this is a lightweight in the world of spookdom next to the haunted mansions in Dixie." The three women got out of the car and stood on the sidewalk at the base of three steps leading to the front door. Dottie Faye took out her ghost-hunting camera and snapped photos while Emma dug through her purse to find her notepad and pen.

Kelly stared at the house. "You know I don't believe in ghosts, but it sure looks like this house has been sitting under a cloud and perpetual thunderbolt for about two hundred years," she said. "Do you suppose the Williamsons forgot to repair the house and maintain the yard?"

"I have no idea," Emma said. "Perhaps we'll find out shortly."

Emma led the way to the front door and rapped on the door three times. She turned to Dottie Faye. "Now remember, no talk of ghosts in front of Mrs. Williamson and Devlin. We are here to get information to clear Vanessa, not do a paranormal documentary."

Before her aunt could reply, the door slowly opened about six inches. Emma could see a round face with a button nose peeking through the crack. "Mrs. Ruth Williamson?"

"Yes," replied a soft, rather high-pitched voice. "Who are you?"

"It's very nice to meet you. I'm Emma Cotton. And this is Kelly Grace and Dottie Faye Sinclair." Emma paused and took a deep breath. "We're looking for Devlin. Is she here, by any chance?"

The door opened wider. "Did you know Devlin?"

"We're friends of a friend. We're hoping she can help us."

"Oh, I think maybe you should come in and sit down." Mrs. Williamson backed away from the door and opened it enough to allow the women to enter.

She ushered the trio into a dimly lit room crammed with old but obviously fine-quality furniture cluttered with framed photos, pieces of crystal, porcelain figurines, and other knick-knacks set atop dainty lace doilies. Everything looked as if it had been untouched for a century.

"Now, which of Devlin's friends sent you?" Mrs. Williamson said after Kelly, Emma, and Dottie Faye had taken a seat on the sofa. She sat in what was obviously her favorite chair, a heavy, well-worn leather piece with a purple-and-pink crocheted afghan thrown over the back. She propped up her feet on a matching ottoman.

"Vanessa Nelson has been accused of a theft she says she didn't commit. She's asked us to help her prove her innocence," Emma explained. "We heard Devlin knew Vanessa several years ago, and we wondered if she could shed any light on Vanessa's background."

The older woman's face clouded and tears welled in her eyes. "My Devlin died five years ago of a heart condition the doctor said was brought on by stress. Vanessa's gossip caused a lot of that stress." She paused, grabbed a tissue from the box on the table by her chair, and dabbed the tears before they could fall. "I think my daughter died of a broken heart."

Emma was speechless. Dottie Faye pulled her duffel bag closer to her feet.

Kelly broke the long silence. "We're so sorry for your loss. I have children and I can't imagine how difficult it must be for you."

The older woman smiled wistfully. "Thank you. You're so kind."

She picked up a porcelain picture frame from the tobacco stand by her chair and gazed at the photo of a young woman sitting in an outside café. "This is my Devlin during her year in Paris before she started working at the museum in Maine. Wasn't she beautiful?"

Mrs. Williamson held out the frame for her visitors to see and Emma rose to take it from her. The slim, dark-haired woman in the photo was smiling, her eyes twinkling as if she'd found the secret to life. "Yes, she was very beautiful."

"My Devlin was born with a heart condition, but she lived a healthy lifestyle. It didn't give her any trouble until she fell in love with her boss at the museum in Maine. The gossip was senseless, really. Both of them were unmarried and Devlin was looking for another job when the rumors started." She paused and watched Emma pass the photo frame to Kelly. "The board of directors got wind of the gossip and forced Jack, her boss and the love of her life, to let her go."

Mrs. Williamson's hand fluttered to her heart. "I believe his choice to not stand up for her hurt more than the humiliation of losing her job. She had lost Jack too."

"What a tragic lost-love story," Dottie Faye sniffed, pulling a hankie from her bag and wiping a tear from her eye. "I don't think I like this Vanessa person very much."

"I miss my Devlin every day, but I don't harbor any ill feelings for Jack or Vanessa, or anyone else involved, really. Devlin and I forgave them long before she died." Mrs. Williamson rose from her chair and crossed the room to a smaller sitting area by the fireplace. "This was Devlin's favorite spot to sit with Poe, her black Persian cat. She read her poetry books to him." She ran her hands along the back of an antique love seat. "Her spirit still lingers here, I think, especially here in her corner, as she called it. I take great comfort in her presence."

Emma and Kelly exchanged looks of disbelief. Dottie Faye seemed spellbound.

Mrs. Williamson returned to her chair. "I'm sorry if I made

you uncomfortable. Some people think I'm rather eccentric."

Emma wasn't sure what to say and was relieved when Kelly broke the silence.

"Mrs. Williamson, Vanessa told us she realized she'd been wrong in hurting Devlin and sent her a letter of apology, but your daughter never responded," Kelly said. "Do you remember her mentioning this letter?"

"Yes, I remember." The woman's voice was barely a whisper. "It arrived about six months after Devlin died. I should have responded, but I couldn't. I was still grieving. Will you tell her she's forgiven, and that she was forgiven by Devlin before her death?"

"Yes," Emma and Kelly said in unison.

Dottie Faye grasped her duffel bag and stood. "May I use your powder room? I need to freshen up."

Following the directions Mrs. Williamson gave her, Dottie Faye lugged her duffel bag down the dark hallway. Emma stifled an urge to burst out laughing when the thing banged against the wall and Dottie Faye's very Southern "dagnabbit" filtered into the living room.

Mrs. Williamson smiled at Emma. "Mrs. Sinclair certainly is colorful."

"Oh, you don't know the half of it," Kelly said. "She keeps us amused."

"Yes, I can see how she would." Mrs. Williamson looked again at Devlin's photo and seemed lost in the past. "I do hope Vanessa has stopped gossiping so much. Her words have hurt so many innocent people over the years."

Emma straightened her back. Vanessa had neglected to tell them this bit of information. "Like who?"

Closing her eyes from time to time as if to retrieve information from her memory, Mrs. Williamson told Emma and

Kelly about a man who was found guilty and sent to prison partially because of testimony Vanessa had given at his trial. "She'd identified him as the shooter in a robbery-murder of a store clerk several years earlier. From the accounts I heard, she took great delight in being on the witness stand. I think she rather liked being a star witness."

"What can you tell us about this man?" Emma asked.

"Not much, I'm afraid." Mrs. Williamson looked apologetic. "His last name is Paine, although I don't remember how to spell it, and I think he now runs a faith-based halfway house somewhere in the Boston area. If I remember correctly, he was cleared in a retrial after new evidence was discovered. I believe he had been a member of a gang before he was arrested, but he cleaned up his act afterward through a prison ministry."

Before Emma or Kelly could ask another question, a blood-curdling scream echoed from the depths of the hallway. Dottie Faye flew into the living room with bulbous eyes and out-stretched arms, moving faster than Emma had ever seen anyone move in stilettos. "I saw it. The spirit … it attacked me." Dottie Faye repeated the same words several times. Suddenly she became lucid, almost triumphant, and held up a small camera. "And I have it on video."

A black cat wandered into the room from the hall and crossed in front of the sofa. Dottie Faye jumped, slapped at her legs and screamed again. "No, not the cat too." She bolted out the front door, leaving it wide open behind her.

Emma saw it was time to go and started for the door. "Kelly, would you please grab Dottie Faye's duffel from wherever she left it? We'll meet you in the car." Emma turned to Mrs. Williamson and handed her a business card from the shop. "Mrs. Williamson, you've been very helpful. Please call if there's anything we can ever do for you."

"You're welcome, Emma. Come back anytime." Mrs. Williamson smiled. "Please remember to tell Vanessa that Devlin and I forgive her."

"We'll tell her. Goodbye," said Emma as she walked down the steps to where Dottie Faye waited, fidgeting on the sidewalk.

Emma and Dottie Faye climbed into the Jeep and watched as Kelly hugged Devlin's mother goodbye, then bounded down the steps to the car.

"We need to find a way to help that woman fix up her house," Kelly said as she opened the rear passenger-side door. "She really is a sweetheart. I wonder why nobody has helped her by now."

They pondered the question while Emma cruised downtown Salem for a place to eat lunch and make notes about what they'd learned from Mrs. Williamson. "Uh-oh, not again," Emma said. "I think we're being followed."

"I think you're jittery because of Mrs. Williamson's creepy house." Kelly turned around and looked through the back window. "Emma, it's an orange compact. How menacing could it be? Whoever it is certainly isn't trying to be invisible."

"It's the black cat. That thing is evil and I have the video to prove it." Dottie Faye held up the camera as proof.

"I fail to see the connection," said Emma as she pulled up to the Sailwind Café. "But I'd still like to take a look at that video after we order lunch."

They settled into a booth, debated the lunch menu, and gave their order to the apron-clad server. Digging into a basket of fresh bread, Kelly pointed to Dottie Faye's camera. "We're ready to watch your video now."

A smug Dottie Faye pressed the play button and pushed the camera closer to the edge of the table so they could all see it. After a minute of fuzzy footage, the video revealed a bedroom packed with dark Victorian bedroom furniture, frilly curtains, and antique dolls with eerie porcelain faces.

"Dottie Faye, I don't see anything remotely resembling a spectral being," Emma said. "Although the odd faces on those dolls are a little unsettling."

"Just wait. It's coming." Dottie Faye leaned forward. "Right now."

Dottie Faye smiled with anticipation as the video showed the black cat benignly grooming itself on top of a pile of boxes next to a large wardrobe. The smile vanished when a bat swooped down from the curtain rod. She stared wide-eyed as she watched the cat leap toward the bat, sending the boxes tumbling. Out of the video frame, Dottie Faye began screaming, ordering the ghost to leave her hair alone. Then the video became a jumble of images and yelling as Dottie Faye ran from the room with the camera running.

Emma and Kelly erupted in laughter as the video ended. "Dottie Faye, whatever would we do without you for comic relief?" Emma asked, her eyes twinkling. "Now, can we please put the ghost talk aside and figure out our next move in finding the person who stole the painting?"

By the time their meal arrived, the women had decided to remove Devlin and her mother from the suspect list and focus on locating the man Vanessa had testified against in the robbery-murder trial. Kelly suggested they stop talking about theft, murder, and ghosts and take some time to visit the Salem Maritime National Historic Site before heading back to Mystic Harbor. Maeve planned to be at the shop all day, so there was no need to be in a rush.

The sun was setting as Emma pulled the Jeep up to Kelly's house. Maeve had called to say all was well at the shop. It was locked up for the night, and Patrick had sent a text message saying Kelly's vegetable soup was warming on the stove and he had bread ready to go into the oven. Emma and Dottie Faye were invited to supper.

"I'm all for a nice, quick dinner and an early bedtime after all of the walking we did today," Kelly said as they strolled to the house.

Dinner was informal and eaten in Kelly's kitchen. Emma successfully steered the conversation away from ghosts and her love life. The women shared their experience at the maritime site with Patrick, and he recounted a phone conversation he'd had with Julie and Keith earlier in the day. After their bowls and the breadbasket were empty, Kelly rebuffed Emma's offer to help wash dishes.

"This won't take long for us to clean up, so you head on home," Kelly said. "I'll see you at the shop in the morning."

"I think I'll actually take you up on it this time," Emma said. "I'm ready to be home."

While Dottie Faye took a trip to the powder room, Emma said good night and walked down the driveway to get the car, keys in hand. Although she had enjoyed the afternoon, she was tired and ready to make a fast getaway.

Emma had just pointed her key fob at the Jeep and unlocked the doors when her free arm was twisted behind her back with a jerk. She felt what had to be the barrel of a gun jabbed deep into her side and hot breath on her ear. "Don't look for what your eyes shouldn't see," a man's voice warned. "It's not healthy."

The man shoved her into the side of the Jeep and was gone before Emma could react. A hawk screamed somewhere in the distance and another echoed a faint reply. Emma jumped into the vehicle, locked the door, and sat shivering in the darkness to wait for Dottie Faye.

fourteen

Emma rolled her head to stretch her neck before dropping several sheets of blank copy paper, several markers, a half dozen index cards, and an information packet into the last of thirty-six brown grocery bags, one for each member of the museum's board of trustees. She must have wrenched her neck trying to twist out of the grasp of her assailant. Stuffing the bags for the board of trustees meeting was a welcome mindless task as she babied her neck and tried to decide what type of sleuthing to do during her shift. After straightening the bags so they were in six even rows of six, Emma decided it was time for a coffee break and snooping. This was her third day of volunteering and she was ready to find some answers.

She stopped in the break room and filled a Styrofoam cup with steaming coffee, added a splash of cream, and held it between her freezing hands. The museum was kept at a low temperature to help preserve the artwork. Somehow, being cold outside never bothered her, but indoors she'd get chilled to the bone if the heat wasn't high enough. She tentatively took a sip and the coffee warmed her inside and out.

In search of sunshine, she strolled into the atrium and saw Jake at the door to Vanessa's office. He appeared to be checking the yellow tape still sealing the area. *Maybe I can ask him a few questions*, she thought, picking up her pace as she approached him. "How's it going?" she asked. "Any news about Vanessa and the theft?"

Startled by her voice, Jake dropped his clipboard, sending

it crashing to the floor. Caught off guard, he lost his balance and stumbled into the line of tape, snapping it.

"Oh, Emma, I didn't see you coming." He bent down to retrieve the clipboard. "I was checking to make sure nobody disturbed the security tape."

Emma smiled at the irony of his words and wondered if he was even aware of what he'd said. "I was taking a little coffee break to stretch my legs and warm my hands." She held the cup to her lips and took a sip. "Are you OK?"

"Yes, I'm all right, except now I have to reseal this office. I've never seen security tape snap like that." He picked up the dangling end of the tape and tried to stick it to the wall, but it fell.

Irritated that he hadn't answered her question about Vanessa, she tried another tack. "You know, I was watching a mystery movie last night about a jewel heist from a museum. The thief turned out to be a former boyfriend of one of the museum's board members. It's amazing how he figured out the security system."

"Oh, our security system is top-notch. I don't know how anyone could have gotten around it," Jake said.

He would have sounded like a braggart if the comment hadn't been so silly. Obviously somebody had gotten around it. Jake was boyishly handsome, but something told Emma he wasn't smart enough to be much of a help in solving the mystery. Emma made a show of looking at her watch. "Well, my coffee break is over. It was nice talking to you."

Emma returned to the administrative office and spent the rest of the morning shredding old papers to be recycled, another mindless task enabling her to concentrate on other things, like finding Mr. Paine. Finding the ex-con was her next objective. When she'd put the last sheet of her fourth stack of papers through the shredder, she tidied up her work space and signed out on the log kept outside Marta's office. "I'm heading out," she said to the public relations director through the office's open door. "I'll see you next week."

She took the stairs to the first floor and crossed the lobby toward the gift shop to find Kelly, hoping she was ready to go.

"Why are you so interested in Vanessa and the stolen painting? You don't even know her, yet you keep asking everyone questions." Emma didn't remember the name of the volunteer who was questioning Kelly. She wondered if the conversation would lead to more information, so she stood outside the door of the gift shop and listened.

Kelly paused long enough before answering for Emma to be concerned. "We bonded over quilts," Kelly finally said. "The pieces in her office are gorgeous."

It was a lame response but probably the best Kelly could do under the circumstances, Emma thought. She stepped into the shop. "Kells, we don't have time to solve every little mystery in the world like when we were kids," Emma said, hoping her chuckle would lighten the mood. She looked at the faces of the other gift shop volunteers. "We've been amateur sleuths since we were in elementary school. We played cops and robbers in the backyard. We also read every Nancy Drew book we could find." Emma tapped Kelly on the shoulder and pointed to the door. "We need to get going. We have a shop to run, remember?"

"She's so bossy. See what I put up with?" Kelly grinned as Emma pushed her out the door. "See you next week."

Kelly almost stumbled into Jake, who was now standing outside the door, obviously eavesdropping.

"Is everything OK?" Jake asked.

Emma nodded. "Everything is great except we're late getting

to the shop. We have work to do—work that pays the bills and allows us to volunteer."

She hurried Kelly out of the museum to avoid anyone else questioning their curiosity. As they crossed the lot to the volunteer parking area, Emma told Kelly about her earlier conversation with Jake.

Kelly sighed. "Here I was gearing up to play matchmaker because he was so cute, but I can't see you with someone that obtuse."

"Well thank you. Dottie Faye does enough matchmaking. I don't need you to start too."

When they were several yards away from the Jeep, Emma unlocked the doors with the remote. She was ready for a speedy getaway. Slipping into the driver's seat, Emma put the key in the ignition and was about to start the car when Kelly yelled her name.

"Emma, I think you'd better come and look at this."

"What now?" Emma said, getting out of the car. She walked around the back of the car to where Kelly stood staring at the rear tire.

"Your tire's been slashed."

Emma shook her head as rage swept through her. "Slashed? This thing's been shredded."

"I'll call Mom and let her know we'll be later getting to the shop." Kelly's phone was already in her hand. The phone call was short, but Emma was already getting the jack out of the back of the Jeep. "Emma, it's a bit chilly out here and you're still stiff from that crazy incident. It'd be faster to call your road service and have them take care of this."

"I've changed tires before. It's easy and it doesn't take too long." Emma leaned the jack against the tire.

"I know. I'm asking you as a favor to me. Call the road

service so we can get you a new tire faster. I'm getting creeped out here. The other night you had a gun in your ribs, and today your tire is slashed."

"Ladies, I couldn't help but notice your predicament when I walked out to do my rounds," Jake said. He was walking to the car with a Styrofoam cup in each hand. "I brought you coffee. Whoa, I thought you had a flat. But this—this is a different thing altogether. Is there anything I can do?"

Emma and Kelly took the cups of coffee he offered.

"Thanks, but no," said Emma, pulling out her card holder and cellphone. "I have roadside service through my insurance."

"I'll finish my rounds then. Just let the receptionist know if you need me." Jake nodded and strolled back through the visitors' parking lot.

They sat in the Jeep while Emma called the road service. As soon as she ended the call, her phone rang. "It's Vanessa," said Emma, staring at the caller ID.

"Yes, we can meet with you. We happen to be in Boston right now, at the art museum. Can we meet at The Golden Wok?" said Emma. "We can walk there from here."

Emma and Kelly dumped their coffee out in the nearby evergreen planter and threw the cups in a trash bin in Emma's car.

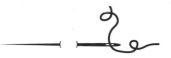

Emma deftly pinched a bite of ginger chicken and a snow pea pod with chopsticks and popped them into her mouth while Kelly described the Jeep's slashed tire with dramatic flair. The food was tasty and she hadn't realized she was so hungry. But she was anxious to move the conversation on to another subject, such as the reason Vanessa had wanted to meet with them.

She swallowed the chicken and snow pea and waved the chopsticks in the air as if directing a symphony. "Do you think anyone suspects we are investigating the theft for you? Any suggestions on who might have done this?" Emma watched Vanessa's reaction to the question. She didn't see anything amiss. She decided to keep the gun incident secret for the time being.

"No, but I do have some information for you." Vanessa leaned into the table and lowered her voice. "I've been doing what I can from home to clear my name. On a whim, I tried logging into the museum's intranet and discovered the museum had not removed my security clearance."

Emma's eyebrows raised and Kelly's jaw dropped.

"That's lucky for us, but it doesn't give me a lot of faith in the museum's security practices." Emma sipped her hot tea. "It certainly leaves plenty to question about the opportunity a thief would have had to penetrate the security system."

Vanessa's hair fell dangerously close to her plate and she brushed it aside. "There's more. When I logged into the security system, I discovered that during Claire's leave of absence, someone was using her access code to bypass security and enter the collection storage area."

Kelly jiggled in her chair. "Who had access to Claire's code?"

"Very few people, actually. Gabe Lucier, Kayla Turner, Jake, and me."

"Jake? I can't see him as the thief," said Kelly. "He doesn't seem smart enough to have pulled off a heist."

"Well, I did catch him outside the door to Vanessa's office today. He said he was checking to make sure nobody disturbed the tape, but the goofball ended up ripping it himself." A surprised Emma had Vanessa, the ice queen, and Kelly laughing in unison.

When the laughter subsided, the women ordered another pot of tea and considered the others on Vanessa's list.

Kelly, who had already polished off a plate of sweet-and-sour pork and a side of egg rolls, cracked open a fortune cookie and asked about Gabe Lucier. "I've not really seen that much of him. He doesn't exactly hang out in the gift shop. What's he like?"

"Smart. Harvard smart. And his family is wealthy. I don't know what his motive would be," Vanessa said. "Why would he steal a painting under his own watch? His job is in jeopardy having one stolen from the museum."

"And Kayla?" Emma paused as the server poured them fresh cups of tea and scampered away. "I've only spoken to her in passing. What about her?"

"Kayla's an institution around that place," Vanessa said, picking at the half-eaten food on her plate. "She's been there forever and knows where all of the skeletons are buried, including mine. But we've worked closely together over the years. She wouldn't frame me because I know where hers are buried too."

Because she didn't know what to say, Emma took a long drink of water. She didn't understand a friendship, if that's what it was between Kayla and Vanessa, based on fear.

Kelly looked at Emma and slapped her hand on the table. "Oh my goodness, in all of the excitement over the tire and the security code, we forgot to tell Vanessa about Devlin Williamson."

"What about her?" Vanessa pushed away the remnants of her Szechuan shrimp and veggies. "Does she still hate me?"

"She never hated you," Emma said, surprised to see what appeared to be concern in Vanessa's eyes. "Mrs. Williamson said Devlin had forgiven you before she died five years ago."

Vanessa looked from Emma to Kelly. "So that's why she never responded to my letter. She never received my apology."

"Yet she had forgiven you just the same," said Kelly. "That means something."

"It does." Vanessa looked at her watch. "Look, I need to get going. Would you like me to drop you by the car repair place?"

Emma shook her head. "No, that's OK. We can walk."

"Actually, I'd really like to ride with Vanessa." Kelly smiled at Emma. "The excitement has tired me out."

They paid their respective checks, and with very little small talk, Vanessa dropped Emma and Kelly off to pick up the Jeep. Kelly promised Vanessa they'd keep in touch, but no plans were made for the three women to meet in the future.

"Well, that was interesting," Kelly said when they were finally alone in the Jeep. "She seems a bit more human to me now after seeing her reaction to Devlin's death."

"A little, maybe. But remember she is the one bribing us with information to get us to clear her name. I still don't trust her." Emma squeezed the back of her neck with the fingers of her right hand. "Is it really only three thirty? It's been a long day."

"Emma, drop me off at the shop and head home. I'll visit with Mom, and we can close up the shop. You look beat."

Emma returned her hand to the steering wheel. "I'm OK."

"You don't understand, my friend. I'm not asking you. I'm telling you this is what we are going to do. I'd love some time alone with Mom anyway." Kelly gave Emma a look she must have learned from her mother.

"Well, I suppose I could use some quiet time to search the Internet for Mr. Paine. Would you go ahead and put Gabe, Kayla, and Jake on the suspect list?"

When Emma pulled into her driveway, she had to admit to herself she was relieved to be home. A cup of hot herbal tea and a quiet evening alone were what she needed to relieve the tension in her neck. She was unaccustomed to being tired and sore, and rest wasn't an activity she particularly enjoyed.

She hung up her coat, stopped by the kitchen to put on the kettle for tea, and headed to her bedroom to change into comfy clothes. The house was quiet, and it seemed odd to be home before nightfall this time of year.

Emma entered the kitchen as the kettle whistled. She fixed a cup of tea and ambled down the hall to her office, cup in hand. If she found Mr. Paine online fast enough, maybe she'd have time to work on her comfort quilt for awhile.

"Now, Mr. Paine, where are you these days?" Emma asked aloud as she pulled her chair up to the old rolltop desk and opened her laptop computer. "And how did you go from prison to the ministry?"

Emma always loved the creaks and groans in her old cottage, but facing a number of intruders while investigating Rose's death had made her jumpy. Normally calm and rational, she didn't care for feeling skittish one bit. As the laptop booted up, Emma lined up several CDs in the player ranging from classical music to folk rock songs. Music blocked out the odd noises and enabled her to concentrate.

Returning to the computer, Emma tried several search variations of the words *Payne, Paine, shelter* and *Boston*. No luck. Then she added *ministry, faith-based*, and *Salem*. Halfway through a CD featuring folk musicians with ties to New England, Emma struck gold when she found a listing for New Life Shelter located on the Mystic Harbor side of Boston, about twenty miles away. The director was listed as Vincent Payne. After jotting down a few notes about the shelter and important dates included on the website, Emma bookmarked the page and closed the computer. She sat back in the chair and looked from the desk clock to her quilting basket on the floor beside the love seat. For the first time in months, she had time to work on her comfort quilt. She enjoyed having several quilts in progress at one time—a quilt to help her relax at home and another to work on while socializing at the Nimble Thimbles meetings, along with projects for Cotton & Grace.

Emma nestled down in the love seat and removed pieces for a single block of the double wedding ring design. She felt the stress leave her body as she carefully pulled each tiny, uniform stitch through the curves of a ring. Minutes slipped by and Emma realized the CD player had stopped and her eyelids had begun to flutter.

After returning the material to her quilting basket and padding to her bedroom, Emma turned off the lights and crawled into bed. She drifted off to sleep thinking of the irony that her comfort quilt—the project she treasured most because it kept her relaxed and sane—was traditionally made by or for brides. The last thing she wanted to be at this point was a bride.

fifteen

Arriving at the shop Tuesday morning, Emma was surprised to find Kelly sitting at the register nearly hidden by three medium-size boxes of new supplies. "Wow, you're here early. Is the world coming to an end?"

"Not yet, luckily. Patrick had a meeting this morning, so we were up and about early. I decided to come in and catch up on things," Kelly said, pulling packages of batting from a box. "We promised to not let things slide when we started investigating Rose's murder, but we've been out of the shop a lot lately."

Emma put her purse in the back room and returned to the counter to help unpack supplies. "I'm sorry I was late, but I'm relieved you were here early. I took an extra-long run this morning to work off the stress of the last couple of days. A nice, easy run always helps work out the kinks." She opened the largest of the boxes to find several bolts of fabrics in new spring colors. They reminded Emma of the small, round fruit candies kids ate by the pocketful. "These are gorgeous."

She took the fabric bolts to the design area, slid them into empty slots on the shelves, and resumed unpacking the box, which also included several packages of thread spools. "During my run, I kept thinking about the slashed tire. The more I thought about it, the more it bothered me. Maybe I should have called the police."

Kelly nodded. "You still can, you know. So far, we've not been hurt worse than a few bumps and bruises, but this could turn dangerous—or deadly."

"I see your point," Emma said. "I'll think about it after we straighten up the shop."

When the boxes were unpacked, Kelly continued recording and putting away the remaining stock while Emma swept the floor and dusted the shelves. Emma wasn't pleased with the dust she found, but she felt a sense of satisfaction by getting rid of it. She preferred to keep the shop and her cottage clean and orderly. "I think I found our ex-con online. His name is Vincent Payne; that's Payne with a *Y*," Emma said. "His program is called New Life Shelter. It's located on the far side of Salem. He started it over three years ago."

"Why do I sense another day out of the shop in our near future?" Kelly said, breaking down the last of the boxes.

"We have to see this through, Kelly. He's a former gang member. Remember? He definitely has a background for theft and a motive for setting up Vanessa."

Kelly groaned. "I know, I know. We'll soon have to offer Mom a job. She's been here more than we have lately."

Kelly was on the phone with Maeve to arrange for her to cover the shop during their trip to Boston when the shop bells jingled and Marta Singh-Moon stepped through the door. Not wanting Marta to overhear the conversation, Emma nodded toward the back room. Kelly smiled and disappeared with her phone in hand.

"Marta, how nice to see you," Emma said, crossing the showroom to welcome her volunteer supervisor into the shop.

"Likewise," said Marta as she glanced around the room. "I was lunching at the Hawthorne House with a friend and decided to stop by to see your shop. It's lovely."

Thankful she and Kelly had taken time to spruce up the shop, Emma showed Marta around the showroom and explained the dual nature of the business, design and restoration.

The items in the showroom, she explained, were largely for display, although a few were usually put on sale at the end of each season. Marta seemed interested in their designs, especially a cover for an electronic tablet she thought would be a perfect birthday gift for her niece.

She seemed particularly impressed when she found copies of *Unexpected Quilting*, a book of quilt designs Emma and Kelly had recently published. "I had no idea you were published designers. We should carry this in the museum gift shop, especially when we have fiber art exhibits running."

As Emma led Marta into the design studio, Kelly joined them while in the process of pocketing her phone. "Marta, thank you for coming by to see our little shop. I apologize for taking so long on the phone. I had a quick matter to handle. I'm all yours now."

Emma unfolded the church bicentennial quilt and spread it across the worktable. "Here's a restoration project in progress," she said, a hint of pride in her voice. "Look at this square; see how the stitching has come loose and the batting is showing?"

Although Marta nodded, she didn't seem too interested. Emma continued her explanation anyway. "Compare that square to this one, which Kelly spent a day on restoring last week."

"Very nice," Marta said and turned to Emma. "Jake Allen told me about your slashed tire. Did you file a police report? Police involvement isn't necessary in this situation because we've hired extra security."

Emma looked directly into Marta's eyes. She knew the woman was simply doing her job by trying to protect the museum. She also suspected her concern was more for the museum's reputation than Emma's well-being. "No, I've not filed a police report. Although I might if my insurance requests me to in order to be reimbursed for the repair."

Marta looked away but quickly turned her gaze to Kelly. "Jake mentioned you've been asking gift shop employees about Vanessa and the theft. Why are you so interested?"

Ah, Emma thought, *now we're getting to the real reason for Marta's visit*. It had nothing to do with her burning desire to see Cotton & Grace quilt designs.

"Honestly, Emma and I have been hooked on mysteries since we were kids. We even had a fingerprint kit and a message decoder," Kelly said. "We probably would have grown up to be cops if we hadn't caught the quilting bug as teenagers."

"That's true," Emma said, running her hand along the church quilt. "We're amateur sleuths and love a good mystery almost as much as old quilts."

Marta took a deep breath and turned to the bolts of fabric lined up behind her. She bounced the index finger of one hand along the top of each bolt until she reached the end of the shelf. "I've decided to trust you, but make sure you don't betray that trust," she said, pivoting slowly to face them. "The museum is in the middle of negotiating the installation of one of the most exciting bodies of work in its history."

Marta paused. Emma figured it would be senseless to ask for details about the exhibit, so she waited for Marta to continue.

"The thing is," Marta said, her voice as icy as morning frost, "any public hint of security breaches or acrimony inside the museum will hinder the finalization of this deal. Do you understand?"

"Yes," Emma and Kelly said in unison. Emma restrained the urge to salute the woman.

Kelly fidgeted. "Marta, why is Vanessa a suspect in the theft? She seems to have a good reputation as far as her work goes. We've heard about her penchant for gossip, but that hardly makes her a thief."

Marta's face looked serene except for a tiny flare of her nostrils. "She has secured a position with another museum. So, you see how her loyalty could be in doubt. Now that I've answered that for you, you must stop asking questions. We have an entire team of professional investigators working on it. We don't need you two interfering."

Emma hesitated. Was she ready to make such a promise? Marta was asking them to be trustworthy, but could they trust anything Marta said?

Silence was heavy in the room. Marta drummed her long, lacquered red nails on her gray silk shirt. "Volunteers may be necessary, but they are a dime a dozen. And the museum carries a lot of weight in the greater Boston area."

Emma knew they were boxed in, and it infuriated her. But she held back her anger. "We understand."

"We'll keep it to ourselves," Kelly added.

"Good. I'd expect nothing less," Marta said as she began making her way to the door. Just as she reached for the handle, she turned to face them once more. "We never had this conversation."

Emma and Kelly stared in stunned silence as the shop door eased shut. When the bells stopped jingling, Kelly escaped to the back room and returned with a large heart-shaped box.

"I suspected on Valentine's Day we'd need some intense chocolate therapy at some point before we solved the art theft mystery," Kelly said, pulling off the lid and holding the heart to Emma. "I'd say this is a good time to break out the stash."

sixteen

"Are you sure we're not on another planet?" Emma said the next morning, stepping around a pile of filthy clothing with what looked like a hypodermic needle sticking out from one side. "A needle on the sidewalk and a burnt car on the street. There's no telling how many times I've been to Boston, but I've not seen anything like this."

"We've led a charmed life, Emma, despite the weirdness we've experienced lately." Kelly looked at the slip of paper in her hand. "We're on the right block. We lucked out finding a place to park so close to the shelter."

Emma's nostrils burned as smoke billowed out of the open doorway of the Hide Away Bar, and a drunk ambled away in the other direction. She wondered what sort of criminals were hiding away in that bar at one o'clock in the afternoon. Coughing, she waved her hand in the air. "If we were truly lucky, we'd have escaped the smokestack."

"No, we're really lucky," said Kelly, pointing at a sign in the next window. The window and the sidewalk outside it were clean, a stark contrast to the surrounding area. "There's the shelter. We made it here walking the two blocks from the car without getting mugged."

The sign was makeshift and primitive, but the thick hand-written letters were neat and legible: "New Life Shelter." Emma gazed at the cardboard promise of a new life. "How many people do you suppose have actually gone on to make a new life after spending time in this place?"

"I have no clue." Kelly pushed open the door and led the way into a large, spotless room filled with two rows of six six-foot tables. Additional folding chairs lined the walls on either side. A bulletin board filled with worn notices took up part of one wall. Beneath it, a square wooden table held a stack of small Bibles and a framed print of Jesus knocking on a door.

There didn't seem to be anyone in the place.

"Hello?" Emma called in a louder-than-normal voice. "Anyone here?"

They walked to the back wall and peeked through the double swinging doors and found an apron-clad, gray-haired man washing dishes. He was cleaning a chopping knife under a faucet in the huge stainless sink. Emma pushed the door open. Not wanting to scare the poor man while he had a knife in his hands, Emma cleared her throat and raised her voice. "Hello, excuse me. We're looking for Vincent Payne."

The dishwasher looked up, turned off the water, and placed the knife in the silverware drainer. "I'm sorry, I didn't hear you. Come in," he said, wiping his hands on the apron before offering a handshake. "I'm Dario Diaz, chief cook and bottle washer."

Emma grasped his hand and smiled. Mr. Diaz had a kind face. "I'm Emma Cotton and this is my friend Kelly Grace. We're looking for Vincent Payne. Is he around?"

"He isn't here. I expect him back in a couple of hours or so."

"We'd like to speak with him about volunteering at the soup kitchen," Kelly said, also shaking his hand.

Stifling a gasp, Emma nudged Kelly's arm. What was she doing? They didn't have time to volunteer anywhere else, especially another place in Boston involving almost an hour of round-trip driving time.

"I'm happy to give you an information packet, but that's

about all I can do. Vincent is in charge of all operations, including the volunteers," said Diaz, his thick accent a hybrid of Hispanic and Bostonian influences.

Emma was torn between the need to get back to the shop and an overwhelming desire to wait for Vincent Payne to return. She didn't want to take any more time than necessary because Maeve had spent so much time at the shop lately, but yet she hated to return to Mystic Harbor empty-handed.

"How long have you worked here, Mr. Diaz?" Emma said in an attempt to keep the conversation going.

"Call me Dario, please. Several years. I started out coming here for one meal a day when I lost my job as a construction foreman. Then two, breakfast and dinner. When my drinking had gotten out of hand and I'd started picking fights during dinner, Vincent pulled me aside and gave me a dose of reality: Straighten up and quit drinking or find another place to eat. He took me to an AA meeting and I did. It wasn't as easy as it sounds."

"I'll bet not," said Emma, reading the man's expression. He sure seemed sincere.

"Vincent took the time to care, and I was smart enough, or desperate enough, to listen. Stories like that are a dime a dozen around here."

Dario led Emma and Kelly out of the kitchen and offered them seats at the nearest dining table. He excused himself and left through a side door. Before Emma and Kelly could say anything, he'd returned with two packets labeled "Volunteer Information." He continued his story as if he'd never left. "He found me a part-time job and things got better," he said. "When I went full time, I started volunteering here on the weekends. And when I retired six months ago, I came back here to help out."

Kelly's eyes filled with tears. "That's some success story, Dario."

"Yes, and I owe it all to the good Lord and to my good friend Vincent. God changes lives here."

Two middle-aged women dressed in torn jeans and old T-shirts came in, removed their coats, and headed toward one of the doors to the left. "Morning, Dario. We'll take care of the bathrooms."

"That's fine, Roberta, Paula. Thank you," Dario said just before the door closed behind the women. "Those two lived here for a while until they found jobs, pooled their money, and found a room to rent. They come here for meals, and on their days off, they clean our bathrooms and sometimes the sleeping quarters."

Emma nodded. "Success stories come in various ways, I suppose—"

"Oh, my achin' back," said a familiar voice with a really bad fake Boston accent. "I'm in a bad way, I tell you. Where's the man of God? I need some prayin'."

Kelly, facing the door, had already seen the spectacle that was Dottie Faye masquerading as a homeless woman and was obviously struggling to restrain a smile. Emma twisted in her seat, eyes widening. This was a new look for her aunt. The normally teased hair was matted in blond clumps sticking out from under a skull cap. The knees of her faded jeans were torn, and her flannel shirt was wrinkled and buttoned crookedly. A shabby men's coat topped off the look. Dottie Faye stopped her moaning long enough to send a triumphant smile to Emma and Kelly before asking for the minister again. Emma was glad Dario spoke first.

"Vincent isn't here right now. May I help you? I'm Dario."

"But I'm in dire misery and need to talk to him," said

Dottie Faye, her Southern accent peeking through while she batted her eyelashes. "I'm homeless and hungry, and I need his inspiration."

Emma couldn't take it any longer. Much more out of Dottie Faye and she was either going to burst out laughing or slap her and say, "Snap out of it." Neither was a viable option. She smiled at Dottie Faye instead. "My friend and I will get you some food. We were finishing up. And Vincent isn't here right now, so you can come back to see him with a full stomach."

Dottie Faye's eyes widened. Emma knew she had caught her off guard. "Why, why, that's very nice of you."

Dario nodded in agreement. "Yes, it is. Vincent will likely be gone a couple of hours. You have time."

Kelly stood up and put her hand on Dottie Faye's sleeve. "Come on, you poor thing. We'll get you something to stick to your ribs. I'll even throw in a bit of chocolate."

"Did you say chocolate?" Dottie Faye looked at Dario. "I think I'll take them up on their kind offer."

"Dario, thank you. We'll come back to see Mr. Payne another time," Emma said, standing to push her chair under the table.

"You're welcome. Come back anytime, all of you," he said.

Emma and Kelly ushered Dottie Faye out of the shelter and hustled her down the block before speaking a word. Emma pounced as soon as the Jeep was in sight. "Whatever possessed you to come here, and how did you find out where we were?"

"I went to the shop to see you and I found Maeve instead. The irritating little Irish woman wouldn't tell me where you were." Dottie Faye stuck out her bottom lip. "So, I went to your cottage and snooped around until I saw the printout about Mr. Payne and the shelter. I figured you were here."

"Where did you get the duds?" Kelly asked. "Somehow I

can't quite picture those in your closet. Have you ever worn a flannel shirt before?"

"Never. And I never will again," Dottie Faye said. "But I sure was tickled to find it at the Mystic Harbor Community Church Thrift Shop."

The trio drew catcalls from a group of men warming their hands by a trash-can fire. Emma cringed and picked up her step. "Dottie Faye, where's your car? You'd best hop in the Caddy and get back to Mystic Harbor before one of these guys takes a liking to it. I hope you still have some hubcaps."

"It's a bit past your car, sugar."

Emma's stomach rumbled. She hadn't taken time to eat her usual hard-boiled egg and bowl of oatmeal before leaving the house and had instead nibbled on a few grapes. "I'm ready to head back and get something to eat. My fruit didn't last too long," she said.

"I'll buy you a nice, warm meal of your choice if you'll tell me what you're up to," Dottie Faye said.

"I'll bet you would," Emma replied. "But no thanks. After we make sure you're in your car safely, we'll head straight back to the shop. We have work to do."

They walked past Emma's Jeep to the Cadillac.

"Emma, Dottie Faye is offering us a good deal. I think we should take her up on it. We can stop in a mom-and-pop place before we get on the interstate. We're all hungry," Kelly said. "What do you say?"

"I don't like it when you two double-team me. Dottie Faye, do you really want to be seen looking like that? It's not your style."

Dottie Faye laughed, tossing her head. "It's not like anyone will recognize me anyway."

"Touché. Where would you like to go?"

Kelly gave Dottie Faye directions to Shelly's Place, a neighborhood restaurant they'd passed on the way to the shelter. "It's three or four miles down the road. It looked like a safe area. We can stop there before we get on the interstate." Kelly dug her phone out of her purse. "I'll call Mom and see if she'd like us to order her carryout."

"Dottie Faye didn't see this, but I snapped a photo of her in that thrift store getup at the restaurant," Kelly said as she and Emma entered Cotton & Grace. They paused as the door closed, looked at the photo, and erupted into laughter.

"You two sound more chipper than Kelly did earlier on the phone. What's so funny?" Maeve said from behind the register counter.

"You gotta see this." Kelly held her phone up for her mother to see. "Recognize her?"

Maeve squinted and leaned closer to the phone. "No. It can't be. Is that Dottie Faye in one of her disguises?"

Emma and Kelly held Maeve spellbound as they recounted Dottie Faye's grand entrance at the shelter.

"Emma, I know you were frustrated when Dario said Mr. Payne wasn't at the shelter, but the trip was worth it to see Dottie Faye in what could have been her best disguise and worst acting job yet," said Kelly, a loud snort accompanying her laughter.

The three women chortled in unison. They were still laughing when a deliveryman walked in with a shoe–box–size package addressed to Emma and Kelly and held out a clipboard and pen for a signature. Kelly composed herself long enough to scrawl her name on the log while Emma accepted the package.

"This is awfully light," Emma said to the deliveryman, giving the box a little shake. "Are you sure there's something in there?"

"I couldn't say." The man smiled and took the clipboard from Kelly. "Have a good one."

"You too," the women said in a chorus. They watched the door close behind him.

"Did we order anything else?" Emma asked. "I thought everything came in earlier this week."

"I thought so too. But we'll find out soon enough. Go ahead and open it." Kelly strolled to the register counter and returned with a box cutter. "These might help."

They sat down at the worktable with Emma in the middle. Maeve and Kelly leaned in as Emma snipped the tape on the box and carefully lifted the lid. She pulled back the soft black fabric lining the package and gasped. "What in the world?"

"Bird bones," said Maeve. "That would be a bird skeleton."

The room fell silent for a few seconds.

"I think it might be a good time to call the police," said Kelly.

Emma thought of the most recent string of odd events—the prowler, Alex Manning's warning, the slashed tire, and the times she was followed while running and driving. She looked at the skeleton nestled in the velvety material encasing it like a shroud. A chill started from the base of her neck and shot down her spine.

"Yes," Emma said. "This time I agree with you."

seventeen

Emma woke with a start and rubbed her eyes. Her fitful sleep had been filled with a montage of ski masks, dark cars, slashed tires, and colorful birds suddenly emaciating into skeletons. She needed a distraction, something to pop her out of this skittish mood. Despite the investigation and strange events surrounding it, she still had work to do and a business to maintain. She needed to calm down. For the first time in ages, she didn't feel like running. She needed something to soothe her soul.

Her heart was still pounding when she took her yoga mat from the bedroom closet and carried it to the great room. She turned on her soft, relaxing music, unrolled her mat on the floor, and took three cleansing breaths before easing down to her hands and knees into the cat-cow pose. Holding this pose for about a minute, Emma felt her heart rate slow and her mind calm. All thoughts of bones and guns slipped away as she moved into the downward-facing dog position and on to the rest of her yoga routine. The music hugged her as she stood straight and raised the sole of her left foot to her right inner thigh while placing her hands together in a prayer pose. Emma felt strong, balanced, and centered in the tree pose.

A loud pounding on the front door destroyed Emma's peace and knocked her off balance and out of the tree. Her heart rate shot up and warm breath erupted from her nostrils. Frozen on her mat, she contemplated what to do. The pounding started again. Emma took a deep breath, and she shook off the fear and surprise. *I've got to regain control. I'm in my own home, the door is locked, and whoever is on the other side of the door clearly isn't trying to sneak up on me.*

She crept to the front door and peered out the peephole to find Kelly pacing back and forth, clutching a paper bag and two cups of coffee. "Boy, am I glad to see you," Emma said, throwing the door open and taking one of the cups from Kelly's grasp.

"Wow, that was a hearty welcome," Kelly said, stepping through the entryway. She gazed at Emma and frowned. "You look like you've seen one of Dottie Faye's ghosts."

"Hardly." Emma took a sip of coffee. "Thanks for the java. To what do I owe the honor?"

"Mom called and said she was up earlier than usual and offered to open the shop so we can get to the shelter early this morning. She thinks we'd have a better chance to catch Vincent Payne before noon."

"What would we do without her?" Emma motioned toward the kitchen. "Let's sit in here and eat."

They sat at the small antique oak table in the breakfast nook and discussed their day, a quick trip to Boston and relieving Maeve as early as possible. Kelly downed a jelly-filled doughnut and an apple fritter. "I wonder if Dottie Faye will materialize at the shelter this time."

Emma picked at a plain cake-style doughnut. Her fitful sleep had robbed her of an appetite. "I'm not so sure I could take another performance like the one she gave yesterday, at least not with a straight face," she said. "I haven't told her when we were going to return to the shelter."

"That's true, but we didn't tell her about it yesterday, either. She showed up anyway."

"Yes," Emma replied. "And on that note, I'll go get cleaned

up and leave you to surfing the Internet on your phone and digging up whatever you can find in the refrigerator."

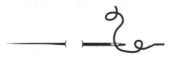

Emma backed the Jeep into the one parking spot left on the block and felt her grip on the steering wheel loosen. "Our luck continues. The only parking place available in a three-block radius happens to be in front of the shelter."

"I admit, I'm relieved," Kelly said. "It was unnerving walking by the catcalling men at the trash can fire yesterday."

"I try to not let things faze me, but I do feel a bit out of place in this neighborhood. Please don't mention the volunteering thing again, OK?"

Before Kelly could respond, Emma's cellphone chimed. "It's Eric."

"Well, answer it."

Emma hesitated a second before she pushed the talk button. "Good morning, Eric."

"Good morning yourself. How are you?"

Emma watched a bedraggled old man lumber up to the shelter door and open it with bare fingers sticking out from holes in his gloves. "I'm fine, thanks. Kelly and I are in Boston. What can I do for you?"

"I'm hoping you'll have lunch with me tomorrow. Are you free?" Eric said. "I thought we could go to The Hawthorne House. I have the afternoon off, and I can't think of a better way to spend it."

"Yes, sure," Emma said, her eyes fixed on the shelter door. "What time?"

"I'll stop by the shop at one o'clock, if that works for you."

"Yes, OK. I can do that." A young couple entered the shelter with a baby stroller. Emma wanted to get inside the shelter and find Mr. Payne before more people arrived. "I need to go now, Eric. I'll see you tomorrow. Goodbye."

"I'll look forward to it, Emma. 'Bye now."

"Woo-hoo." Kelly leaned over and gave Emma a playful shove. "You actually have a date. You're getting soft in your old age."

"It's not a date. It's just lunch. Can we please go see Mr. Payne now?"

Kelly grinned and opened her door. "Yep, we sure can."

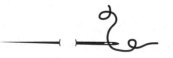

A few stragglers from breakfast remained at the tables while two rotund women resembling gnomes cleared large stainless steel pans and bowls from the L-shaped serving area. Their voices echoed across the nearly empty room. The young man and woman with the baby had stopped by the small table and were thumbing through a copy of the Bible. Emma and Kelly walked toward the kitchen to ask about Vincent Payne when Dario ambled through the swinging door.

"You came back," Dario said, his eyebrows arched in surprise. "How did your meal go yesterday? That was very nice of you to take the time to feed a stranger."

"She was a trip, that's for sure," Kelly said.

"Yes, she was." Emma looked around the room, looking for someone who looked like he could be the shelter director. "Is Mr. Payne here?"

Dario bobbed his head. "He's in his office. I'll tell him you're here. And feel free to sit down anywhere."

Emma and Kelly sat at the table closest to the door Dario had taken to find Mr. Payne and watched as the remaining tables cleared, one person at a time. The old man with the holey gloves took his trash to the garbage can by the kitchen and turned toward the door. He stopped in front of them on his way out, his mouth spreading into a toothless grin. "Aren't you gonna eat? The food's really good here."

"It sure smells like it," said Kelly. "But we're just here to see Mr. Payne."

"Vincent. He's a good man, yes he is." The toothless grin bobbed up and down. "You get some food now."

"Thank you," Kelly said as the old man shuffled away.

They watched him step into the sunshine and pause on the sidewalk, as if deciding which way he should turn.

"I see you met Nathaniel." The voice came from behind them. Emma and Kelly turned to find a short bulldog of a man with ebony skin stretched by muscles along his collarbone and biceps bulging under his red short-sleeve T-shirt. "He was one of the best saxophone players in Boston back in the day, before alcohol ruined his career. He battles the bottle, but he still loves music and people."

"You must be Mr. Payne." Emma held out her hand. "I'm Emma Cotton, and this is my friend and business partner, Kelly Grace."

"Yes, but please call me Vincent. Dario said you came by yesterday and asked about volunteering." He shook hands first with Emma and then Kelly. "Thanks for your interest. Did you read the information he gave you?"

"I did," said Emma. "It looks like you do good work here, and on a shoestring too."

"Yes, by the grace of God we're able to serve so many in this neighborhood. I grew up here, so it has special meaning to me."

Emma searched his face for remnants of his gangland past and effects of prison time, but she found none, save the scar that dimpled the skin under his jawbone. His brown eyes held wisdom and peace under eyelashes almost too long for a man's face. "That's some scar you have there."

He ran a stubby finger down the length of the puckered scar. "Before God saved me from myself and the gang life, I spent time in prison for a crime I didn't commit. But I expect you knew that already, didn't you?" Vincent stared into Emma's eyes. "You're not here to volunteer, are you? Why don't you tell me the real reason you wanted to see me."

Caught off guard, Emma hesitated long enough for Kelly to answer him.

"We heard about your trial and prison time from someone who followed your case," Kelly said. "It must have been difficult spending years in prison, an innocent man convicted on testimony from someone you'd never met."

"Prison was hard and it left more scars than the one on my face, but I changed when I was set free and given another chance. I forgave Vanessa Nelson, the woman who testified that she saw me shoot a man, a long time ago. It was the only way I could cleanse my heart for this ministry." Vincent looked across the room to the crew now cleaning tables and sweeping the floor and smiled. "I don't begrudge the time I spent in the pen. I may not have pulled the trigger of the gun that killed the store clerk, but I'd been on the wrong side of the law and hurt my share of people."

Emma and Kelly listened quietly as Vincent told the story of his time spent in the gang, his arrest and trial, and how he'd found his way to God through the prison ministry.

"I'd found redemption in prison and I promised myself and God if I was ever released, I'd spend the rest of my life helping others," he said. "When the real murderer was caught and confessed, I was released and God brought me here—to this inner city war zone—to minister to others who'd misplayed their hand in life."

The room fell silent as the work crew finished cleaning the dining room, and most of them disappeared into the kitchen. Only one man remained to replace notices on the bulletin board. Emma wondered how much she should tell Vincent about Vanessa. Her gut told her he was on the level and was telling the truth. "Vincent, in a strange twist of irony, Vanessa is now being accused of a crime she didn't commit. Kelly and I are sort of amateur sleuths. We're trying to help her."

Vincent's forehead wrinkled as his eyebrows tensed. "Ah, I get it now. You thought I might've had something to do with it," Vincent said. He smiled. "I've no need for retaliation. I'm a free man doing work for God. I wish I had some helpful insight to offer, but I never really knew Vanessa. We both happened to be near the store when the robbery went down. The only time I ever saw her was inside the courtroom."

"That would have made most people angry and bitter," Kelly said.

"I was angry and bitter for a long time. She obviously reveled in being in the center of the trial and played the role of witness to the hilt. I came to realize she wasn't intentionally hurting me; she honestly thought her testimony was truthful. I knew she had made a mistake. I felt I had to forgive her and let go of the anger." Vincent's eyes drifted from Kelly to Emma. "The main reason we forgive as Christians is because God has forgiven us. It releases us from bitterness and anger and allows us to move on with our lives."

Vincent stood up, took a card out of his wallet, and handed it to Emma. "Here's a list of references I give to everyone interested in volunteering or donating to the shelter. Feel free to check them," he said. "I must get back to work. I'm sorry I've not been much help to you."

"Thank you for sharing your story with us," Emma said, handing him a business card. "If you can think of anything that might shed light on why someone might want to frame Vanessa for theft, please call me."

"I will. Contact me anytime I can help," he said.

When Vincent had disappeared through the side door, Emma and Kelly walked to the shelter entrance. The man who was sweeping leaned his broom against the wall and followed them outside.

"Hey, you two," he said, getting close enough to make Emma back up a couple of steps. "Listen up: Vincent is a good man who helps a lot of people. It wouldn't be so good for your health to be bringing trouble his way. Got it?"

"Yes sir," Kelly said, grabbing Emma's arm and pulling her to the Jeep. "We got it loud and clear."

eighteen

"Oh no you don't." Maeve held the broom like a lance and seemed ready to jab the stick end into Dottie Faye at a moment's notice. "You're not touching that quilt."

"I don't want to touch your precious quilt. Go back to your sweeping and leave me be, old woman." Dottie Faye stood, eyes blazing, on a step stool with a shirt box in her hand. "I brought some decorations of my own to share with the girls. Just a few trinkets to liven up the place."

Emma and Kelly stood in the door of Cotton & Grace and watched the battle unfold. Kelly shook her head. "They're at it again. Shall I break it up this time, or do you want to do the honors?"

"Be my guest." Emma made a sweeping gesture with her left hand. "Break away. I'd really like to get back to work on the church quilt."

Taking several steps into the room, Kelly clapped her hands five times in rapid succession. "Mom! What are you doing? I've not seen you wield a broom like that since you found Kathleen, Sean and me as kids eating ice cream right out of the carton."

Maeve stood her ground but her face softened. "I was minding the shop—and my own business—when this one comes in here, moving things around like she owns the place. What was I to do? Let her put plastic dime-store decorations next to fiber-art pieces? I don't think so. And four-leaf clovers don't have the same meaning as shamrocks. No four-leaf clovers."

"Mom, put down the broom, and Dottie Faye, get down

from that stepladder before you get hurt. I have news," Kelly said. She leaned toward Dottie Faye as if sharing a secret. "It's even juicier than *Soap World Love Stories*."

"Alrighty then," Dottie Faye said, stepping off the ladder. "I guess that's a good trade."

Maeve stood silent and still until Dottie Faye had both feet on the ground and had placed the box on the counter, and then she lowered the broom. "So, what's your news?"

"Well," Kelly said, cutting her eyes to Emma, "our Emma has a date."

Emma glowered. "I didn't know you were going to tell them that." But a smile tugged at her lips. Kelly's announcement had been effective in breaking the tension between Dottie Faye and Maeve.

"Spill it." Dottie Faye faced Emma with her hands on her hips. "We want all the juicy details."

"Yes, don't leave anything out," said Maeve, leaning the broom against the wall behind her.

Emma shuffled her feet and ran her fingers through her hair. "There aren't many details to tell. Eric Hart and I are having lunch tomorrow, a casual, very public lunch. It's no big deal, and the less said about it the better."

Dottie Faye grabbed her purse and glanced at Maeve. "I know that look. Emma Jane's digging in her heels. We'll not get any more information out of her today." She walked around the counter and wrapped Emma in a bear hug. "But I expect a full report tomorrow afternoon."

When the door had closed behind Dottie Faye, Maeve gathered her purse and quilting bag. "I need to get going too. I'll come back tomorrow after lunchtime to finish the decorations."

"Thank you for the decorations and the time you've spent in the shop lately," Emma said. "I'm sorry we've been away so much. But we're so grateful to have you to look after things while we're chasing down leads. Otherwise the mystery of Rose's murder might never be solved."

After Maeve left, Emma and Kelly settled in the alcove to resume work on the church quilt. The next hour passed in companionable silence as each concentrated on a different area of the quilt.

"That's it. I need to do something else for awhile," Kelly said, pushing her chair back from the worktable. "I finally finished this one pinwheel. I can't look at this pattern anymore, gorgeous though it may be."

Emma had been wondering when Kelly's short attention span would dictate a change in her activity. While the required focus on details enabled Emma to clear her mind and relax, she knew Kelly found the necessary sitting and tedious repetition of stitching restricting after a short amount of time. "This would be a good time for you to call the references Vincent Payne gave us. I'll continue working on the church quilt," Emma said. "I'm making serious headway on these stars. We might get this quilt done with time to spare before the church's bicentennial celebration."

"Bless you," said Kelly, bounding out of her chair and across the room to the computer on the register counter. "I'll do a quick search on the names to see if they are legit. Then I'll make the calls."

Engrossed in their work, the soothing Celtic music Kelly had piping through the shop was interrupted only by her calls to Vincent's references. Emma looked up in surprise an hour later when Kelly plopped down next to her.

"I called all the references and received glowing reports from each of them," Kelly said. "They were impressive, including a Boston city councilman, the principal of the neighborhood high school, an attorney, and even Mom's old friend, Marlene Mathis, a banker in the city who actually sits on the shelter's board of directors."

Emma rearranged the quilt so Kelly could work on it later in the afternoon. "Are you confident enough to cross him off our suspect list?"

"Yes I am, although part of me wonders if anyone can be as perfect as Vincent supposedly is, especially for a former gang member. But the references were convincing. He really seems to be a changed man."

"I agree." Emma walked to the register counter, pulled a marker from a cup by the computer, and handed it to Kelly. "Here, you checked the references, so you do the honors."

Emma plopped into one of the comfy chairs in the alcove as Kelly disappeared into the storage room to update the suspect list. She closed her eyes and leaned back. Another lead that didn't pan out. It irritated her to think the key to finding Rose's killer continued to be held hostage until the art thief was caught. Why had it been so difficult to clear Vanessa's name? Could she really be guilty?

"Ahhhh, it's amazing what can be done in a morning when we don't leave the shop and the phone stays quiet." Emma closed the bookkeeping program on the computer and glanced at the clock. It was noon already. Eric would be there in an hour, and Emma was relieved Kelly hadn't brought up the lunch date. Emma crossed the shop to check the progress Kelly had made on the church quilt. "How're the stars coming?"

"They're coming along. We'll meet our deadline, especially

if we have more quiet mornings like this one." Kelly spread out the quilt and took several paces back to stand beside Emma. "It really is a treasure."

"The quiet morning or the quilt?" Emma joked.

"Well, I meant the quilt, but the morning sure was productive."

"Yes, it was. And I'm sure your mom is enjoying having a day away from the shop," Emma said.

As if on cue, Maeve opened the door.

"Mom, what are you doing here? We have the shop covered today," Kelly said, giving Maeve a hug.

"I know. I came by to see Emma off for her date with Dr. Hart."

Emma took a deep breath. "It's not a date, just lunch. It's no big deal." She paused when Maeve winced. "But I appreciate your support."

The shop bell jingled and Dottie Faye breezed through the door. "Are you all ready for your big day?" She studied Emma for a moment and frowned. "Sweet pea, you look a bit peaked." Rummaging in her oversize shoulder bag, Dottie Faye pulled out a blush compact and a lipstick tube. "I'll fix you right up."

Emma backed up as Dottie Faye advanced toward her, the compact open and its brush poised for action. "Stop moving or the blush will smear and you'll look like a lady of the night."

"Dottie Faye," Emma said, taking a step back. "I'm old enough to do my own makeup, thank you."

"Well then, put on some more lipstick. It'll make all the difference in the world." Dottie Faye uncapped the tube and held it out for Emma. "Here, try this. It'll bring out the burgundy in your sweater."

"No, thank you. I have my own lipstick."

Returning the makeup to her purse, Dottie Faye took

Emma's arm and escorted her to the alcove where she gently pushed her into a chair. "Now, Emma Jane, you must remember to bat your eyes. Men love that." She proceeded to demonstrate the technique. "Now you try it."

Emma looked at Maeve and Kelly, her eyes imploring them for help. She was dismayed to find them chuckling and taking great delight in the dating lesson unfolding before them. "You two are no help at all."

The chuckles turned into hearty laughter.

Dottie Faye told Emma to hold out her right arm. "Now, to indicate your interest, run your fingers up his arm like this," she said.

Dottie Faye's fingers tickled her as they ran off the three-quarter–length sweater sleeve and onto the middle of her forearm. Before she could stop it, a belly laugh erupted and filled the shop. The laughing fit spread first to Dottie Faye, then Kelly, and finally Maeve. Emma couldn't remember the last time she'd laughed so hard.

They were still chuckling when Eric arrived.

"You ladies look like you're having way more fun than anyone else I've seen today," Eric said as the door closed behind him. "I don't hear too much laughter during flu season, but at least that's tapering off now."

Emma jumped up and brushed several strands of hair from her eyes. How much of their teasing had he heard? "I'm ready. I'll grab my coat from the storeroom."

When she returned, Eric was staring at the shamrock quilt Maeve had made. "I see you're all ready for St. Patrick's Day. My great-grandfather Hart was Irish, so I grew up celebrating the holiday. The quilt is really something."

"Maeve made it for me," Emma said as she shrugged into her coat. "Isn't it lovely?"

"It is. My Hart relatives would approve." Eric looked at Emma. "Are you ready? I thought we'd walk. It's unseasonably sunny and warm today. We should enjoy it while we can."

Eric put his arm lightly on Emma's back as they squeezed between occupied chairs while following the waiter to their table. Every few paces, one of Eric's patients would wave or tap his arm as he passed. Was it her imagination or were all eyes in the room watching them? Relief washed over Emma as she sank into the chair Eric had pulled out for her at a small corner table.

Although she already knew she'd order the spiced walnut chicken salad, Emma picked up the menu and pretended to read it while she tried to think of something to say. She considered several openers, like asking him about his favorite entrée on the menu or if he'd ever been here on nights when they had live folk music.

"Do you come here often?" she asked instead.

"That's supposed to be my line," he said, his eyes twinkling with mischief.

Emma felt her face flush. Why hadn't she asked about folk-music night? "That didn't exactly come out right, did it?"

"Not exactly, but I liked hearing you say it." Eric smiled and opened his menu. "I eat here once in a while. Riley really likes their spaghetti. I'm more of a steak guy."

"I'm more like a rabbit," Emma said.

"Somehow I expected that." Eric looked up as the waiter approached the table.

"Hello, Dr. Hart," the black-clad young man said as he filled the water glasses. "Are you ready to order?"

After they'd ordered their meal—a spiced walnut chicken salad for Emma and the French dip sandwich for Eric—Emma relaxed into the conversation. Her nerves calmed as they discussed running, a hobby they shared, and the new Downtown Merchants First Friday events scheduled to start in April. How had she not noticed how easy he was to talk to?

Eric was, with great animation, filling her in on the upcoming Annual Jazz Festival held each April when she heard a familiar voice travel from the other side of the potted plant. "Now, be a dear and take this back to the kitchen and bring me something stronger." The Southern accent was unmistakable. "I declare, I've not had a decent glass of iced tea since I arrived in Mystic Harbor."

"Eric, if you will excuse me, I need to freshen up a bit before our food arrives," Emma said, forcing a smile. "I'll be back in a minute."

Emma took off in the direction of the ladies' room, but once she was sure neither Dottie Faye nor Eric could see her, she doubled back and crept up behind her aunt. Dottie Faye was partially obscured by the plant and completely focused on watching Eric through a mini-camera. Emma bent down and put her mouth next to Dottie Faye's ear. "Enjoying the show?" she asked loudly.

Startled, Dottie Faye jumped up and flailed her arms wildly, bumping into the potted plant, which fell over onto the decorative column beside it. "What show? You've been away from the table."

"It's time for you to go. Now." Emma picked up the plant and straightened it as best she could.

"But I wanted to see how your date was going. I didn't want to interrupt anything."

"Your surveillance techniques are OK when you're

hunting down mysteries, but not when you're spying on my lunch dates."

"Ah-ha." Dottie Faye grinned. "You called it a date. I knew it was a date."

Emma pointed to the camera. "Put that thing away before the management bans you from the place forever."

A server hurried up to the table, her hands twisting the white apron. "Is everything all right here?"

Emma nodded. "Yes, but my aunt has decided to take her lunch to go. Minus the iced tea." Emma watched the server scamper off to the kitchen. She looked at Dottie Faye. "I'm going back to my table now. Go eat your lunch someplace else. We'll talk later."

"OK, Emma Jane. I'll wait here for my carryout lunch." Dottie Faye winked and sat down, slipping the camera into her purse. "You enjoy your date."

"I will, now that I don't have a camera staring at me." Emma took the long way back to her table so she could compose herself.

When she returned to Eric, their food was already on the table. "Oh, Eric, I'm so sorry. I hope your sandwich isn't cold. I ran into someone I knew on the way to the restroom."

He took a bite of the French dip and moaned in appreciation. "It's not cold. It's perfect, as usual."

Emma drizzled half of the sherry-infused raspberry dressing over her salad and speared a bite with her fork. "I've been spending so much time in Boston lately, it's nice to sit down and eat in my favorite restaurant in Mystic Harbor."

She looked around the dining room and felt at home among the colonial-style furnishings and portraits of the area's founding fathers. Even at lunch, the flame of a small oil lamp flickered next to colorful flowers in a bud vase on each table. She loved the ambiance of The Hawthorne House.

"How are things at the museum?" Eric dipped his sandwich into the au jus. "Dottie Faye said something about an uptight woman holding information of some sort hostage. Those were her words. She has quite a way with them."

"That she does," Emma replied with a chuckle. "She's actually been a big help with the investigation."

Emma updated him on the investigation of Rose's murder. She found herself enjoying the role of storyteller and noticed how his nose twitched slightly when he laughed while she recounted Dottie Faye's haunting at the dilapidated old house in Salem. His eyes didn't stray from her face as she talked, although they did widen when she told him about the slashed tire and the bird bones.

"Emma, I know better than to ask you to stop investigating Rose's murder, but please tell me you are at least keeping the police updated when things like this happen."

"Well, I did report the box of bird bones. That was creepy," Emma said. "But I don't want to wear out my welcome with the PD. Deputy Chief Boyer already thinks I'm obsessed. I sure don't want to make things worse."

Eric reached out and covered Emma's hand with his own and gave it a light squeeze. "You seem to rattle cages a little harder with each suspect. Please be careful, and let me know if I can help in any way."

Caught off guard, Emma pulled her hand away and looked at her watch. "I will, thanks. But now I really need to get back to the shop. Kelly and I have work to do."

"I understand," Eric said, putting his hand up to signal the waiter. He had his wallet ready when the young man returned with the check. He handed the young man several bills. "Thanks for the excellent food and service, as usual. Keep the change."

They wound their way through the maze of tables with few

stops this time. When they walked through the heavy wood door and down the steps, Emma enjoyed feeling the sun on her face, although the air was still cool. They strolled through the town square on the way back to Cotton & Grace. "The tulips and crocuses should be blooming soon," Emma said. "I've always loved the square in spring."

"Me too," Eric said. "A lot of times I'll bring my lunch out here to eat once the weather warms up."

When they crossed Gallows Way in front of Cotton & Grace, Emma saw Dottie Faye peeking out the door, a hand over her head to block the sun's glare. With her aunt hovering, she knew a fast getaway was necessary or she'd never hear the end of it.

"Thank you for lunch. I enjoyed it very much," said Emma. As she turned to grasp the shop door with one hand, Eric grabbed her other one and held it a moment.

"Take care of yourself, Emma. Please." He squeezed her hand, let go, and took a couple of steps toward his office before he turned around. "And Emma? Tell Dottie Faye we all enjoyed her comic relief today." Before she could react, he winked and continued walking down the sidewalk, leaving Emma staring in embarrassment.

Eric wasn't six paces away before Dottie Faye threw open the door and pulled Emma inside. "He squeezed your hand, didn't he? He's so smitten with you. I can see it in his eyes," said Dottie Faye, dropping Emma's hand to clap several times in a short burst of excitement. "But you will really know it when he kisses you."

Maeve brushed Dottie Faye out of the way. "So, how did lunch go? I mean, once you got rid of the spy in the bushes. Dottie Faye told us all about that."

"We talked about the upcoming First Friday events, the

food, running, and the investigation into Rose's murder. He was very nice." Emma opened her mouth to add something but caught herself before she said it.

"And? I heard an 'and' in that hesitation of yours," Kelly said.

Emma felt her cheeks redden. "And I suppose I could possibly be persuaded to have lunch with him again, should he ask."

"Oh, sugar pie, he will most definitely ask," said Dottie Faye grabbing her purse. "I'm off to get a manicure. My work here is done."

The shop was quiet for a moment after the door closed.

"I'm out too," Maeve said. She retrieved her bag from below the register counter. "It's nice to see you enjoying yourself, Emma. You need to do it more often."

"I do enjoy myself, but thank you for the moral support." Emma placed her hand on Maeve's forearm. "I appreciate you."

After Maeve and Dottie Faye left, Emma and Kelly stood in the center of the shop, taking in the quiet stillness. Before Emma could step away, Kelly turned to her quickly and wrapped her in a hug. "Emma, I'm very proud of you."

nineteen

"This place is quickly losing its charm for me," Kelly said, holding the staff and volunteer door open for Emma as they left the museum. "There was a definite chill in the air today, and it wasn't from the weatherman."

"Yep, for me too." Emma glanced behind them to make sure their conversation was private. "Marta gave me a to-do list and went over it with me, but she didn't say another word all afternoon."

"Doreen Hallinan called Mom last night to tell her we're ruffling feathers. Our volunteer status is definitely in jeopardy. One of Doreen's friends on the board of directors told her they were afraid news of the theft will be leaked to the press." Kelly stopped in her tracks. "Do you suppose that's why they changed our shift to the afternoon? Because we had talked so much to volunteers in the morning?"

"All the more reason to find out who stole the painting so we can get the information from Vanessa and get back to finding Rose's killer. This has taken too much time away from the shop anyway." Emma clicked her key fob and unlocked the doors to the Jeep when they were about four cars away. "I've been thinking. We need to look into Vanessa's ex-boyfriend. I know she said he'd not be involved in something like this, but he sure was livid at the hospital gala. Obviously, he has some animosity."

Emma had parked under a leafless tree along the far side of the volunteer parking lot because it was the only space open when they'd arrived. Given recent strange incidents, including the tire slashing, she'd been leery of parking so far away from the entrance. She approached the Jeep with caution. As Kelly went to the passenger side, Emma walked past the rear of the car, peered around the barren tree to make sure no one was hiding, and let out a breath before hurrying to the driver's door. As she reached for the handle, a hawk darted from a tree branch, shrieking as it disappeared into the darkening sky.

Heart pounding, Emma jumped into the car and started the ignition. "I've never been the excitable sort, but now even screeching hawks are unnerving me."

When her breathing and heart rate slowed, Emma backed the Jeep out of the space.

"Emma, stop!" Kelly pointed across the parking lot to Jake's reserved space by the entrance. "What's Jake doing at his car before his shift is over?"

The security guard bent over the open car trunk, but Emma couldn't see what he was doing. Without warning, he stood up straight, glanced around the parking lot, and removed a bulky bundle from the trunk. Struggling under the weight, he walked back inside the building.

"Somehow I don't think storing and moving bulky items is in his job description," said Emma.

"I'm not in too big a hurry to get home, and I do believe one of us left a purse in the building. Don't you think so?" Kelly looked at Emma. "If you pull around to the front, we can go in the public entrance and slip up the stairs."

"Now that you mention it, I'm not quite sure where my purse is at the moment. Thanks for reminding me," Emma replied. She pressed the accelerator a bit harder than usual and whipped her trusty Jeep around the museum. They entered the building just as Cammie Smythe was locking up the gift shop.

"Hi Kelly, Emma. Kelly, do you need anything out of the gift shop before I lock up?" Cammie stood with the key in the lock.

"No; actually, Emma left her bag upstairs and didn't realize it until we were about to pull out of the parking lot. We figured it'd be faster to come in the front, if it was still open."

Cammie nodded and turned the key. "I'm not sure why Jake hasn't been around to lock up. It's about that time."

"Yes, we'd better hurry before the administrative suite is locked," Emma said, tugging Kelly's arm.

As they turned the corner, the elevator doors were closing behind Jake.

When the elevator lifted from the ground, Emma and Kelly dashed to the stairs.

"Emma, slow down." Kelly paused to catch her breath about halfway up the flight. "We don't want to be exiting the stairwell as he's getting off the elevator."

"You're right, I suppose. That elevator is really slow." Emma stopped while Kelly caught up with her. "But I don't want to take so long that we have a hard time finding him."

Emma forced herself to walk the rest of the flight. She eased the door open and stuck her head out to see if anyone was in the hall. "All clear," she whispered to Kelly. They crept down the hall, past the classrooms and Vanessa's office. A few doors from the administrative suite, angry voices blasted into the corridor from Claire's office.

"Jake, what did you do?" Claire's voice was harsh.

"I did it for you. For us."

"Jake, there is no 'us.' We're co-workers, nothing more."

Emma and Kelly looked at each other. They'd found Jake, all right, and Claire too. Emma felt like they were listening to one of Dottie Faye's soap operas. She inched closer to the door, motioning Kelly to follow.

She heard a rustling and a light thump. "But I took the painting for you."

"You did what?"

"I took the painting and hid it in my car. It wasn't hard to make it look like Vanessa had done it. All I had to do was plant the inventory sheet documenting the painting's value and *bam*. Instant suspect."

He sure did sound smug, Emma thought. She was tempted to peek in the door to see the look on Claire's face, but she didn't want to risk being seen.

"You put a $100,000 piece of art in the trunk of your car?" Claire's voice was tinged with disbelief. "But why would you do such a thing?"

Kelly tapped Emma on the shoulder and pointed to her phone, indicating she'd been recording the conversation. Emma gave her a thumbs-up and leaned forward so she could better hear what was happening in the office.

"I love you, Claire. I know how disappointed you were when Kayla hired Vanessa as assistant curator over you. I wanted that job for you." Jake seemed reluctant to take a breath. "Don't you see? If Vanessa was caught stealing a painting, she'd be fired, and then you'd finally have the job she stole from you in the first place. And that condescending ice queen would get what she deserves."

"Why?" Claire's voice trembled when she started to speak. "Why did you choose now to tell me all this? And why did you bring the painting to me? Why not put it back in the collection and conveniently 'find' it?"

Emma could tell Jake was pacing around the room. It sounded like he was becoming more agitated. She couldn't tell exactly where Claire was inside the office.

Emma stole a quick glance as Jake pounded his fist on the

desk. "I'll tell you why now, because something's not right about those two new volunteers, Emma and Kelly. They ask too many questions and are into everybody's business. I know what they're doing. They're trying to discredit me because the painting went missing under my watch."

Wincing, Emma looked back at Kelly. Kelly's eyes widened, and she shook her head with a frown. But Claire's next words made them smile.

"I think you're wrong about them. I thought that at first, but they're fiber artists, quilters. I heard they grew up taking art classes here." Claire's voice sounded a little stronger. "They seem to love this museum. That's why they've asked so many questions."

Another loud noise blasted into the hallway as Jake's frustration level rose. Emma startled. Was he beginning to lose control?

"No! You're so naïve. I've been watching and listening. I know everything that goes on in this place," Jake said. His diabolical laugh made it sound like he was losing his mind. "But I took care of them. They've not been snooping as much since I started tailing them. I even followed Emma on her morning runs. I know her habits now. I scared the wits out of her when I slashed her tire. You should've seen the look on her face when she saw that."

Emma's jaw dropped. Jake slashed the tire? But he'd seemed so concerned about their safety at the time. She shuddered.

"You're crazy, that's what you are. I'm calling Gabe now. He left, so he can't be too far away." Claire's voice was filled with desperation.

"Put your phone away. Please, baby, put it down," Jake cooed. A scuffling sound broke his words momentarily. "You have to listen to me. I love you."

"Jake, take your hands off me this instant."

Claire was sounding more forceful. But so was Jake. Emma had heard enough. Thankful she had input all the museum staff numbers in her phone, she sent Gabe a text message: *Crisis in Claire's ofc. Plz return.* His reply arrived in seconds. *On my way. 3 min max.* Emma showed Gabe's response to Kelly and pointed to the office. "It's time to go in," she whispered.

Emma had started carrying Mace after the gun incident in Kelly's driveway, so she dug the canister out of her purse and slipped it into her coat pocket for quick access.

Emma pushed her way inside first. "Jake, step away from Claire, and we'll tell you why we were asking so many questions. Yes, we were looking for answers, but the questions had nothing to do with you."

Jake pulled his gun from its holster and jammed it into Claire's side. "Don't lie to me. I know what you were doing. I know everything that goes on around here. But how did you find out?"

For a moment, the room was silent except for the sound of four people breathing more heavily than usual. Kelly spoke first. "OK, I give. What did we find out?"

Jake laughed. "Now you're acting innocent. But I know you've been snooping. The Greenville Police Department had no right to fire me." He tightened his grip on Claire and waved the gun at Kelly. "I was a good cop—not dangerous, like they said."

"No, of course not," Kelly deadpanned.

Emma grimaced at the sarcasm, but Jake had obviously missed it. They needed to calm him down. It wasn't the time for jokes. "Jake, we were trying to clear Vanessa of stealing the painting because she'd been a friend of our childhood pal Rose, who died a long time ago." Emma's voice was soft and controlled as her hand tightened on the Mace can in her pocket, her index finger on the spray button. "We were doing it for Rose."

Jake relaxed his grip on Claire but kept the gun in her side. He seemed to be considering Emma's words. "You weren't investigating me?"

"No. Ironically, Kelly was trying to get me to go out with you, weren't you?"

Kelly nodded but didn't say a word.

"Me? A date with me?"

"Yes." Emma cringed at the lie.

"I was so bad to you." Jake shook his head. "I cased your house, slashed your tire, followed you during your runs. I even sent you a casket of bird bones—a stroke of genius on my part. All for nothing?"

Emma let his words soak in and took a step forward. "You forgot the time you shoved the gun into my side at Kelly's house. You jammed it in the same spot where you have it on Claire now."

Looking confused, Jake pulled the gun away from Clair's side. "What? I never went to Kelly's house, and I've never even had a hand on my gun around you until now. What do you mean?"

Nostrils flaring, Jake released Claire and shoved her to the side, then took a step toward Emma.

Feelings of rage swept through her. She'd had enough. Without the slightest hesitation, Emma jerked out the Mace and pressed the button, spraying the chemical squarely into Jake's eyes. A rush of adrenaline ran through her as the security guard dropped his gun and fell to the ground, groaning and clawing at his eyes. She stepped closer and kicked the gun out of his reach.

Kelly raced to Claire's side and put her arm around the

shaking woman's shoulders. Emma kept her Mace pointed at Jake and mentally pleaded with Gabe Lucier to walk in the door.

Jake still writhed on the floor with his hands over his eyes when Gabe rushed in with his five-man security team. Emma, Kelly, and Claire were escorted by Gabe and a member of the team to Kayla's adjoining office.

Once Gabe was convinced the three women were unharmed, he sat down behind Kayla's desk. Emma, Kelly, and Claire sat across from him. Mac, the security team member, stood by the door.

"Now that I know you're all right, will someone please tell me what is going on here?" Gabe looked at each of the women. "The police will be here shortly. I called 911 as soon as I heard the scuffle. Now, start from the beginning," Gabe said, settling back in his seat.

"Better yet, you can hear the whole thing," said Kelly, fishing the phone out of her pocket and placing it on the desk. "I recorded it."

Gabe nodded. "Even better."

They listened silently as Jake lost his grip on reality.

Sitting with her hands in the jacket pockets, Emma's fingers brushed against the Mace can. Thank goodness she'd had it with her. What would have happened if she hadn't? She shuddered and forced the thought out of her mind.

Soon after the recording ended, two men in Boston Police Department uniforms entered the room, identifying themselves as officers Pratt and Mason. They took statements from the three women and Gabe Lucier. Pratt said two other officers had also arrived and were questioning Jake across the hall.

After giving her statement, Emma winced as Jake stumbled by the door in handcuffs, flanked by police officers. "What's going to happen to him?"

Mason fished business cards from his wallet and handed one to each of them. "There will be an investigation. We'll let you know. If you can think of anything else, please call me."

Gabe followed the officers into the hallway and exchanged a few words with them, but soon returned to Kayla's office.

"If there's anything else you need to tell me, this would be a good time," Gabe said, reclaiming his seat behind Kayla's desk.

An hour later, they'd told him everything about Rose's murder and the investigation, Vanessa's agreement with them, the strange incidents, and Jake's behavior. "If that's everything, I'll escort you out. The museum will handle this. I trust you to be discreet."

As they walked out of Kayla's office into Claire's space, Kelly stopped and looked at the painting still leaning against the wall. She put her hands on her hips and cocked her head. "There's one thing I don't understand."

Every pair of eyes in the room looked at her. "What's that?" Gabe asked.

"Why did he choose such an ugly painting to steal?" she said. "It looks like a three-year-old opened tubes of paint and squeezed it willy-nilly all over the canvas."

The burly security guard chuckled. "I was wondering the same thing."

Gabe and Claire looked at each other with amusement. The museum director shook his head but said nothing.

"Oh, you don't know what you are saying." Claire stepped over to the painting and gestured with both hands. "This was created by one of the most revered abstract expressionists of our time."

Kelly moved toward the door. "I think I'll stick to quilting."

twenty

"I figured I'd hear from you tonight." Vanessa actually smiled as she opened her apartment door and motioned Emma and Kelly inside. "Gabe called and filled me in. Emma, I hear you took Jake down with Mace."

"That she did," Kelly said. "It was quite exciting. You should have seen her."

"I suppose I owe you some information." Vanessa led them into the living room. "Have a seat. I told you I wasn't guilty."

"You did," said Emma. "But your little extortion ploy did nothing to assure us of your innocence."

Vanessa leaned back in her chair and crossed her legs. "Maybe not, but, as the saying goes, desperate times call for desperate measures. Clearly, I was desperate. Innocent and desperate."

Could've fooled me; you sure didn't act desperate, Emma thought as she stood to take off her jacket. She placed it over the back of the sofa and sat back down. "So, what can you tell us about the night Rose died? What's this big revelation you promised?"

Vanessa closed her eyes for a second, and Emma wondered if she was doing this for effect or if the ice queen was actually overcome by memories.

"Rose seemed upset and nervous on the last night of class. In fact, she'd been rather agitated and distracted all week," Vanessa said. She looked beyond her guests and seemed to be gazing into the distance—or the past.

Emma and Kelly waited for Vanessa to continue. When the silence became uncomfortable, Emma decided to hurry her along. "Rose was always distracted about something, but usually it was something whimsical and fun," she said. "She didn't get upset or nervous too often, mainly when she saw animals or children mistreated. How does this relate to the big secret you've been hiding?"

"You know, I've never believed Rose's death was an accident. I'm pretty sure she was pushed down those stairs."

Kelly cleared her throat. "Go on."

Vanessa shot Kelly an irritated look. "I had a very egotistical, albeit talented, classmate. His name was Tony Mann, and he was gifted enough to receive a Delaunay Scholarship. His talents far surpassed anyone else's in the class, even Rose's."

Emma was getting frustrated. She got it; Vanessa was jealous of this Tony Mann's talent. Why was this taking so long? "Ego doesn't make a man a murderer, Vanessa."

"Let me finish." Vanessa tossed her head and frowned. "After the last class, I presented the quilt to Rose. She was so gracious and overwhelmed. I could tell she was pleased, even though the quilt squares were rough at best."

She paused and ran her index fingers under her eyes to catch the few tears gathered on her bottom lashes. "She offered to write a reference for me because I was starting my job search. But even then she kept glancing at the door and drumming her fingers on the table. She was definitely nervous about something."

Vanessa rose and paced the floor behind the sofa as if in a trance. "I was in a hurry. After I said goodbye to Rose, I went down the hall to get my other art projects from the semester. Rose always kept them on display throughout the term for all the students to see. That was her way of promoting us as artists, you see."

Emma and Kelly twisted on the sofa so they could see Vanessa. Although she was interested in hearing tidbits about Rose's last minutes, Emma wondered where this was leading. They watched Vanessa meander around the room in a daze.

"When I left, about fifteen minutes after class let out, Tony was holding court with the ladies—he was quite the lothario," Vanessa said with a sneer. "Tony and his groupies were standing at the top of the stairs, the very stairs Rose tumbled down to her death."

Emma's breath caught in her throat. She looked at Kelly, who appeared to be having the same trouble breathing. Somewhere in the depths of the apartment, Vanessa's refrigerator rumbled, but she was silent. Emma waited for more details, feeling like a beggar seeking alms.

Several long moments passed before Vanessa spoke again. She returned to her chair and sat on the edge of the cushion. "I never liked Tony. He was always smug and self-righteous, even to his instructors. To this day, I'm convinced he either killed Rose or he saw something that last night after class." Vanessa leaned so far forward that Emma thought she might slide off the cushion. "But you'll never prove it because of who he is."

Vanessa paused, obviously for chilling dramatic effect. For a split second, Emma hoped the woman would slip onto the floor and snap out of the theatrics.

"Well, Tony Mann—the star of our class and the bane of Rose's existence—is none other than Antonio Roman." Vanessa collapsed onto the back of the chair and seemed to take great enjoyment from watching their stunned reaction to her news. "Yes, the creative genius behind Roman Originals Fabric and one of the most powerful people in the industry quite possibly murdered your friend Rose."

Emma looked at Kelly and was sure their wide-eyed expressions were mirror images of each other. Kelly gaped at Vanessa before returning her gaze to Emma. "Well, she did promise us big news. This is pretty darn big. Stunning, even."

"Yes, she did," Emma said. "And we thought going behind the scenes on Broadway and investigating a star like Kevin Crawford was exciting. But Antonio Roman? It's pretty mind-boggling. Vanessa, we use Roman fabrics in our designs and restoration projects. He's always been among our favorite designers."

"I imagine it will take some doing to get to him. From what I hear, he has an entourage larger than most Hollywood stars, and a self-image to match," Vanessa said. "I wish you luck."

Emma stood up. "Well, you certainly delivered on your promise of big news. If you're right, Kelly and I may soon be starting our last adventure into the investigation of Rose's murder."

Rising to her feet, Kelly held out her hand to Vanessa. "Thank you. It's been a wild ride, but at least we have another clue."

Grabbing their coats, Emma and Kelly said a hasty good night and promised to let Vanessa know when Rose's murder was solved. Overwhelmed by the events at the museum and Vanessa's bombshell, they wordlessly donned their coats and rode the elevator in silence.

The night was cool and relatively quiet for Boston. The rancid scent of smoke still hung in the air, wafting from the burnt building down the street. Emma's mind was filled with dueling thoughts. Part of her wanted to hit the road to New York as soon as possible to find Rose's killer. The other part of her didn't want to leave her cozy home in Mystic Harbor ever again.

They walked down the steps in front of the apartment building and headed toward the car.

"I guess we're off to New York," Kelly said, breaking their silence.

Emma shook her head. "Right now, I want to go home and sleep. No dreams. Just sleep."

A new security guard greeted Emma and Kelly the following Monday when they arrived at the museum for their last day as volunteers. He smiled as he took their names at the door. "Oh, so you're the local heroes. It's nice to meet you."

"I don't know about heroes," said Emma. "but we do tend to stir up excitement everywhere we go."

"That's for sure," Kelly added, laughing. "But I'm ready to have a few less thrills, at least for awhile."

Emma and Kelly entered the building and paused in the alcove by the elevators. "Hopefully, our shifts will run smoothly," Emma said. "I'll stop by the gift shop around noon."

"That works for me. It will be interesting to see what kind of reception we get."

Emma pushed the button on the elevator and watched Kelly torpedo toward the gift shop with her quick, short steps and wondered what trouble they would stir up when visiting New York to investigate the great Antonio Roman.

As the elevator hummed to the third floor and the door opened onto the atrium, she heard a hum of voices coming from Vanessa's office. "Emma," Vanessa called from her desk, "please come in here a minute."

Gabe and Marta rose from the chairs in front of Vanessa's desk. "Thank you for saving the day last week," Gabe said, holding out his hand to Emma. "There's no telling where Claire would be if you hadn't followed Jake back into the museum."

"You're welcome. But remember, it was a team effort. I couldn't have done it without Kelly."

"Please come see me when you're done here. Take your time," Marta said. Her expression and tone were neutral, and Emma couldn't get a read on what she might be thinking.

"Sure, I'll be there shortly," Emma replied.

Marta and Gabe excused themselves. Emma wondered what was left to discuss with Vanessa.

"Since your life had been in jeopardy, I thought you should know what happened to Jake," Vanessa said. She glanced into Emma's eyes. "But you didn't hear it from me, and if it goes outside this office, I'll deny ever saying it."

"Understood," Emma said.

"Good. Not only do we want to try to keep the art theft quiet, we also don't want Jake going to prison. We want to see him get the help he needs. His family and Gabe's go back a long way." Vanessa looked like she was trying to avoid looking directly at Emma, repeatedly glancing at the rose quilt on the wall. "Gabe gave Jake the job as security guard after he lost his position on the police force. His private security team provided the technical aspects of the museum's security. Jake was hired to be an on-site uniformed security presence. Gabe hoped it would help rebuild Jake's self-confidence."

Vanessa finally looked Emma in the eye. "We all knew he suffered from post-traumatic stress syndrome after he was shot in the line of duty, but we didn't realize he was obsessed with Claire or that he had the potential to put anyone in danger. Be assured he isn't a danger to anyone now. His parents put him in a residential facility to help him deal with his issues. He won't ever work in security or law enforcement again."

"Thank you for being honest with me," Emma said. "I'm glad Jake is getting the treatment he needs."

"Claire is too. That's why she didn't press charges." Vanessa nodded and stood up. "I'll walk with you to Marta's office."

The two women gazed for a second at the rose quilt. "You and Kelly make a formidable team," Vanessa said. "I have no doubt you two will find Rose's killer and bring him or her to justice. Thank you for not forgetting her."

They walked quietly to the administrative suite. Emma was surprised to find it filled with museum staff and volunteers milling around a large cake sitting on her worktable.

"You gotta see this, Emma." Kelly was already standing by the cake, ready to pounce once Cammie sliced and served it.

Emma slid through the crowd to take a look and broke into laughter when she read, "Good Luck Emma and Kelly—our most curious volunteers."

"I'd like to say a few words." Marta walked to the cake table and stood between Emma and Kelly. "I know I speak for all of us when I say thank you for the work you've done here—although I'm not sure how you managed to get the donor list updated with your incessant skulking around and interrogating people." She paused to allow the laughter to die down. "And thank you for caring enough to rescue Claire."

Marta clapped her hands a few times lightly and the rest of the room joined her.

"I sure will miss you in the gift shop," said Cammie, handing Kelly the first slice of cake. "But Mom signed up for quilting classes at Uncommon Threads, so I expect we'll be dropping by Cotton & Grace for help quite often."

"Come by anytime," Kelly said, fork poised in midair. "Emma and I are happy to share quilting tips."

Vanessa and Gabe pulled Emma and Kelly away from the cake table.

"We'd really like you to stay on as volunteers," Gabe said. "We sure can use you."

Emma put a bite of cake in her mouth and chewed slowly as she thought of a response. "We really appreciate it, but between running our business and searching for Rose's killer, we are pretty much tapped out time-wise."

"We understand," Vanessa said with a rare smile. "But if I ever need a private investigator, I'm going to give you a call."

Kelly shook her head. "Oh no, we aren't hanging out a shingle as PIs. We're strictly amateurs. But we could recommend a good one for you."

twenty-one

Emma arrived early for the Nimble Thimbles meeting to grab a prime spot on the worktable to begin cutting fabric. Enjoying the calm between solving the museum theft and preparing for a trip back to New York City to meet with Antonio Roman, she spread fabric on the worktable in the quilting room. She'd been able to finish the running quilt by working on it a little bit each day during slow times in the shop and now felt the thrill of starting a new project run through her fingers. Although most of the quilters in the group were transitioning into spring colors, she'd opted for deep hues—green, gold, black, and a hint of maroon.

"Happy St. Paddy's Day," Kelly and Maeve said in unison, bustling into the room and placing two large foil-covered platters on the far end of the table.

"And to you too." Emma put her scissors on the table and went to peek underneath the aluminum foil. "I see you've been busy in the kitchen."

Maeve removed the foil and folded it before placing it in the side pocket of her craft bag. She handed Kelly a package of green and white napkins, and soon the Nimble Thimbles had a small buffet of Irish goodies—Quigley style. They lined up neat rows of water bottles sporting Kelly green ribbons.

"When you solved the museum theft, Kelly had a few days with a bit of free time, so we made good use of them." Maeve said, rearranging the napkins into two fans, one by each platter. "We thought it'd be fun to share."

As the quilters straggled in for their weekly meeting, they gathered by the refreshments, catching up on their week and discussing their St. Patrick's Day plans. Emma looked at the clock. Dottie Faye must have run into another eligible bachelor on her way to the meeting. Should they start without her? She decided to give her a few more minutes. Her aunt would be impossible to deal with if she missed the update on the investigations.

She didn't have to wait long. Dottie Faye breezed in a couple minutes later, clad in Kelly green leggings and a form-fitting white-and-green striped sweater topped with a green feather boa and matching leprechaun hat. "Top o' the mornin' to ya," she said, strutting around the room and obviously waiting for a reaction to her entrance.

She came to a halt in front of the refreshments. "Doesn't that beat all," said Dottie Faye, surveying the platter of Irish soda bread pieces with a tub of butter in the center and the plate of assorted homemade cookies. "Every time I turn around, that woman tries to outdo me."

Emma put her arm around Dottie Faye. "This is Maeve's holiday, so be nice." She handed Dottie Faye a plate. "Have some goodies. And if it makes you feel any better, we waited for you to get here before giving our updates."

After a few minutes of chatting and nibbling, the quilters began migrating to the comfy chairs to work on their individual projects. Emma left her fabric on the table and sank down into a chair next to Kelly to start the meeting.

Breathless from running up the stairs, Marcia plopped into the last remaining chair with Tokala and Walter on either side.

Dottie Faye lugged a folding chair from the table and slid it next to Emma. "OK, everyone, Emma and Kelly have a couple of announcements," she said, introducing them with a flourish. "Take it away, girls."

"You'll be happy to know we're not only celebrating St. Patrick's Day today, but we're also happy to announce we've solved the museum theft." Kelly grabbed her tote from the floor and pulled out a square to complete. "I'll admit we're a bit surprised at the outcome."

Everyone started talking at once, each quilter positive of the thief's identity.

Emma held up her hand. "Nope, you're all wrong."

Emma and Kelly took turns recounting the events leading up to Jake's dismissal from the museum.

"I beg your pardon, Emma Jane." Dottie Faye waved her feather boa in the air. "I wasn't totally wrong. It may not have been a love triangle causing the commotion, but it was unrequited love." She stared at Maeve. "So I guess my idea wasn't as absurd as you thought."

Maeve set the partially completed quilt square in her lap and looked at Dottie Faye, shaking her head. "It was about as absurd as that crazy boa you're wearing. By the way, most people in Ireland don't wear green feather boas on St. Patrick's Day."

Pulling a stitch through a yellow tulip for his daughter's quilt, Walter chuckled. "Actually, I think it's suitably ironic that the person we thought was protecting the artwork turned out to be the thief."

"Bone-chilling, actually," Marcia said, her eyes widening as she shuddered. "Thank goodness Emma had the presence of mind to use the Mace before someone got hurt."

"It was pretty tense there for a while, but it was a group effort." Emma was uncomfortable receiving the credit for apprehending Jake. "Kelly was the first one to notice him taking the painting from the car. And it could have ended badly if Claire had not been so calm or if Gabe had taken longer to get there."

She stood to begin cutting her fabric for the new quilt.

"Emma, aren't you forgetting something?" Tokala leaned forward and raised her eyebrows. "Vanessa's clue?"

"Oh, you aren't interested in that little piece of information, are you?" Emma said, laughing and sitting down.

"So what's the big news she promised?" Walter said. "Inquiring minds really do want to know."

"I'll give you a hint," Kelly said. "One of Rose's students went on to become one of the biggest names in fabrics. Emma and I frequently use his designs."

"It can't be, can it?" Marcia looked at Emma and raised her eyebrows. "If so, I think I'll swoon."

"Well, yes," Emma nodded, knowing Marcia's unabashed adoration of any Roman Original. "The Tony Mann who made a quilt square for Rose's quilt is none other than Antonio Roman."

As if on cue, the quilters began tittering in unison. Kelly whistled to get their attention.

"You might not want to start swooning yet," Kelly said. "Vanessa's version of the great Antonio Roman isn't very swoon-worthy."

"Kelly has a point." Emma looked at Marcia. "The Antonio Roman that Vanessa described is an egotistical ladies' man. The last time Vanessa saw him with a group of girls after Rose's class was at the top of the stairs, the same stairs where Rose's body was found the next day."

"What a way to burst my bubble." Marcia said, shaking her head. "But there's no denying his talent."

Emma stood up again. "Now that we've satisfied your curiosity, may I please get to work on my new quilt project before we run out of time?"

Tokala followed her to the worktable. "I saw your fabric when I came in earlier. Hawk eyes and feathers. Sort of a departure for you," she said. "I couldn't help but notice the Hovering Hawks pattern on the table."

"These birds have been dogging me for weeks. I've seen them everywhere—outside the shop, running, near the museum." Emma held up a piece of fabric to show Tokala the details. "They're fascinating in an unnerving sort of way."

Taking the fabric in both hands, Tokala studied it a moment. "Emma, remember our discussion about the Native American totems?"

"I remember."

"Animals in a person's totem show up when you need the traits they possess. Hawks provide the ability to perceive what others do not." Tokala pressed the fabric between Emma's hands. "Perhaps you need to be less distracted by details and focus on a higher perspective."

Dottie Faye pushed her folding chair up to the other end of the worktable and walked around to Tokala and Emma.

"Emma Jane," she said, putting her arm around Emma's shoulders, "Tokala makes sense. Look at the number of times you've gotten the truth about people during your quest to find Rose's murderer, even after going down rabbit trails."

Tokala smiled. "Keep on the path to truth, Emma. You and Kelly will discover Rose's killer."

"We will," said Emma, packing up her fabric. "But now Kelly and I must be on the path to the shop. We have a long day ahead of us before we can have our St. Patrick's Day dinner with Maeve."

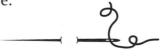

"This is a very nice gesture on your part, Dottie Faye," said Emma, balancing a potted shamrock in one hand while she opened the door of the Cadillac with the other. "Maeve will appreciate a hostess gift. I wish I'd thought of it."

Emma handed Dottie Faye the plant as they strolled up the walkway to Maeve's neat two-story brick home where she and her late husband, Sean, had raised Kelly and her twin siblings. "Ah, St. Patrick's Day at the Quigleys'," Emma said. "Smell the corned beef and cabbage and listen to the beat of the bodhran."

"The beau who?" Dottie Faye asked.

"Bodhran. It's an Irish drum. That's what you hear with the fiddle and Irish pan pipe," Emma said as she rang the doorbell.

"Happy St. Patrick's Day," Maeve said as she threw open the door. "Come in."

Dottie Faye stepped inside, looked around, and extended the potted shamrock to Maeve. "I know how you love to decorate for St. Patrick's Day, so I brought you this. Have you ever noticed how shamrocks are made out of heart leaves?"

"Thank you, Dottie Faye. You shouldn't have," Maeve said. "Kelly, Patrick. Come see what Dottie Faye brought."

Kelly and Patrick walked into the room, their heads bobbing to the music. "Happy St. Pat's."

"Look, you two, Dottie Faye brought me a potted shamrock. Wasn't that nice?" Maeve held the plant out to Kelly with an amused grin. "She even added a Dottie Faye touch—a plastic four-leaf clover with sparkles and 'Happy St. Paddy's Day' on it."

Kelly and Emma wandered into the kitchen to steal a taste of the corned beef. "That was nice of Dottie Faye," Kelly said. "I'm glad Mom didn't say anything about four-leaf clovers having nothing to do with St. Paddy's Day."

They peeked through the kitchen door and watched Maeve and Dottie Faye engrossed in animated conversation while Patrick took the shamrock to the dining room table.

"I know it irritates you, but it's sort of interesting how they put their differences aside in one very Irish tradition," Kelly said.

Emma raised her eyebrows. "Should I even ask?"

"I don't think you need to," Kelly said, chuckling. "For the record, I believe Rose would approve of both our sleuthing and their matchmaking."

Before Emma could reply, the doorbell rang. Smiling, Maeve took measured steps to the door and glanced back into the room before opening the door.

"Happy St. Patrick's Day. Please come in," she said as Eric Hart entered.

Dottie Faye stuck her head in the kitchen door. "You two come out here and wish Dr. Hart a Happy St. Patrick's Day—Dottie Faye–style."

Mystery Sampler Quilt

Create your own mystery sampler quilt with blocks designed by Emma and Kelly and inspired by each book in the series! You'll find a Cotton & Grace block pattern in every Annie's Quilted Mysteries book. At the end of the series, the last pattern will include finishing instructions that will tell you how to stitch the unique blocks together to create a beautiful, one-of-a-kind quilt.

Mystery & the Museum

Mystery & the Museum
12" x 12" Finished Block

Specifications
Finished Block Size: 12" x 12"
Skill Level: Beginner

Cutting

From Light Fabric:
Cut 1 (5¼") square.
    Subcut square on both diagonals to make 4 A triangles.
Cut 2 (4⅞") squares.
    Subcut each square on 1 diagonal to make 4 B triangles.
Cut 1 (4½") C square.
Cut 8 (2⅞") squares.
    Subcut each square on 1 diagonal to make 16 D triangles.

From Dark Fabric:
Cut 1 (5¼") square.
    Subcut square on both diagonals to make 4 E triangles.
Cut 4 (2⅞") squares.
    Subcut each square on 1 diagonal to make 8 F triangles.
Cut 4 (2½") G squares.

Assembly

1. Stitch a G square and D triangle together referring to Figure 1a; press seam toward G.

2. Stitch a D triangle to the adjoining side of G (Figure 1b); press seams toward D. Repeat to make four G-D units.

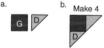

Figure 1

3. Stitch a B triangle to the D edge of a G-D unit referring to Figure 2 to make a block corner; press seams toward B. Repeat to make four corners.

Figure 2　　　　　**Figure 3**　　　　**Figure 4**

4. Stitch a D triangle to opposite sides of E to make a Flying Geese unit (Figure 3a); press seams toward E. Repeat to make four each D-E and A-F Flying Geese units (Figure 3b).

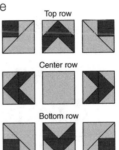

5. Refer to Figure 4 to stitch D-E and A-F units together. Repeat to make four.

6. Refer to Figure 5 to stitch the corner and Flying Geese units and C together to make a top, bottom and center block row.

7. Stitch rows together to complete the block as shown in the block diagram.

Figure 5

HELPFUL HINTS

• Choose light and dark fabrics for this block. Use scraps from other projects or purchase fat eighths (9" x 22") or fat quarters (18" x 22") to make one sample block.

• Cut individual pieces from scraps, or cut strips and then individual pieces from strips if using yardage or large pieces of fabric. For example, to cut several 2½" squares, cut a 2½"-wide strip the width of the fabric. Subcut the strip into 2½" squares.

• Use a ¼"-wide seam allowance for all seams and stitch right sides together.

• For more detailed help with quilting techniques, go to QuiltersWorld. com and choose Quilting Basics under Quilt Essentials, or consult a complete quilting guide. Your local library will probably have several on hand that you can review before purchasing one.

Learn more about Annie's fiction books at

AnniesFiction.com

- Access your e-books
- Discover exciting new series
- Read sample chapters
- Watch video book trailers
- Share your feedback

We've designed the Annie's Fiction website especially for you!

Plus, manage your account online!

- Check your account status
- Make payments online
- Update your address

Visit us at AnniesFiction.com

Annie's Quilted Mysteries™

COMING SOON!

OCEAN SELVAGE

Emma and her friends set sail on the high seas in order to investigate their next suspect, Antonio Roman. Antonio is a popular fabric designer who happens to be the keynote speaker on a quilting cruise. Emma and her friends never expect to get mixed up in an unrelated missing person's case aboard the ship—or to have one of their own named as a criminal suspect!

Can they unravel the mystery and find the answers they seek about the death of their dear friend Rose? Or will a devious culprit run their plans aground?

Don't miss the next book in this exciting new series from Annie's Quilted Mysteries!

Annie's®

AnniesFiction.com